FO
SUMMER,

FOREST SUMMER

by
Mica Ford

First Published in Great Britain in 2018
by Castleman Publishing

ISBN 978 0 9928482 2 4

Typeset at The Spartan Press Ltd,
Lymington, Hants

Printed and bound in Great Britain by
The Dorset Press, Dorchester.

Cover designed by Marion Bayliss

Line drawings by Beresford Leavens

Facebook : Mica Ford - Forest Adventures

FOREST ADVENTURES

This book is dedicated to my family who
have suffered my obsession with
horses with (mostly) patience
and understanding.

1

'Who wants to say hello to the ponies before supper?'
Aunty Anna asked her nieces when they had finished
hugging each other.

'Yes, YES, YES PLEASE,' and off the girls dashed, clat-
tering over the little wooden bridge, racing along the
footpath to the paddock, leaving Grandpa and Granny
to unload the car.

'Calm down, girls! They're already out in the field;
walk quietly so we don't startle them,' Anna called as
she ran to keep up.

Niki, with her long 10 year old legs, climbed the
five-bar gate into the stable yard in one easy stride;
Beth, being shorter, had to scramble up the bars before

jumping down from the top, while Lolly just squeezed through the fence. Niki shushed them bossily and they all walked quietly to the stables.

'Niki, fetch some carrots from the feed room,' Anna said when she caught up. 'They've already had supper but they'll come for a treat.'

Niki took charge, handing out slices of carrot to her sisters and the girls called the ponies' names softly, holding out their hands to tempt them. Bracken, a stocky bay New Forest pony was Niki's favourite and she hugged him, stroking his mane and murmuring to him as he munched his carrot. Beth and Lolly fed and patted Magic, a smaller pretty grey mare of Welsh origin. Lolly had to make do with patting the pony's shoulder and nose as she couldn't reach any higher. The ponies nudged the girls, nibbling with their soft muzzles and gently head butting them for more titbits.

Anna's horse, Summer, came over to demand treats too, pushing past the smaller ponies. Niki, ever the protective older sister, stood between the two smaller girls and the big black horse.

'What sort of horse is Summer? I've forgotten,' Beth said thoughtfully.

'She's big – very big,' Lolly said, moving to stand behind Niki.

'She's a Tracker isn't she?' Niki asked Anna.

'Nearly right Niki. She's a Trakehaner which is a Russian horse bred for its speed and courage. They're very intelligent too, though Summer can be a bit too clever at times, thinking she knows best,' Anna smiled at Niki as she ruffled her hair.

'Now, show them your hands are empty so they can see there's no point in begging for more,' Anna said, and sure enough the ponies ambled away to carry on grazing.

The sunset glowed a rosy pink as they walked back to the house, happily breathing in the fresh country air.

'Right – time for supper, then baths and bed.'

That morning, at the sisters' home in the midlands town of Ashton, Lolly had woken early. Most mornings she would stay under her quilt but not this day. She had sprung up and down on her bed shouting to her sisters.

'Wake up, wake up. We're going to the New Forest today. We'll see our ponies tonight and then it's only one more sleep till our first ride.'

Lolly and her sisters lived with their parents in a terraced house in the suburbs and they loved visiting their grandparents and aunt in the New Forest during the school holidays. Granny and Grandpa's cottage had fields and the open forest on one side, a village and the beach on the other. This summer the girls were staying for the whole school holiday and Aunty Anna had promised they could ride her ponies every day, as well as helping when she took her horse to competitions.

'Sshh,' Niki had opened one eye. 'Be quiet Lolly – you'll wake Mummy and Daddy,' she said.

At ten and three quarters Niki was much more sensible than five year old Lolly and could be quite bossy when Lolly was too bouncy, but this morning was different. Niki grinned when she realised what Lolly was chanting.

She swung herself down from the top bunk, trying not to step onto Beth, who had just celebrated her eighth birthday.

'Oopps, sorry, Beth. Wake up, wake up.'

'Go 'way! I'm still asleep,' she grumbled, turning over and curling into a tight ball.

'Wake up,' Niki tugged at Beth's duvet. 'Granny Elliot's coming today to collect us from school. You and Lolly clean your teeth while I finish packing.'

Beth's eyes sprang open and she sat straight up, just as excited as her sisters once she'd remembered it was the last day of term.

'Come on Lolly,' Beth grabbed her sister's hand and they rushed to the bathroom. The two girls peeped around their parents' door to check if they were awake.

Mummy yawned as Lolly and Beth climbed on the big bed, jumping with excitement. Daddy turned Lolly upside down and tickled her to stop her from bouncing, while Mummy and Beth had a quiet cuddle. Niki joined them after she had finished being grown up and helpful.

During breakfast Daddy rang Granny Elliot to check the arrangements.

'We'll pop over to your house after school, to have a quick tea and collect the girls' bags. It's a three hour drive so we won't hang around,' Granny said. 'I'll ring once we're back. Grandpa and Aunty Anna send their love.'

'See you soon – kiss the ponies before you come – and Charlie dog,' the girls yelled down the phone.

'Bye, see you later,' Granny shouted back.

Granny was waiting in the school yard when the bell rang and children rushed out of every door. Lolly bounced up and down with excitement as she called goodbye to her friends.

'Stand still, Lolly,' Niki grabbed her little sister's shoulders. 'You haven't stopped jumping since waking up this morning,' she exclaimed bossily. 'I think your nickname should be Jack in the Box.'

The girls dozed during the long drive, only waking when Granny said they were nearly there. Three pairs of eyes strained to be first to see the wild ponies and foals and the cows with their calves, grazing beside the New Forest roads.

'Look at that pony with her foal – ahh, it's having a drink,' cried Lolly, pressing her nose to the window.

'Isn't it cute? It looks like a magical unicorn with its cream coat and dark mane and tail. Look, there's another one lying down,' Niki answered.

'Oh, and look at that hairy calf with fur in its eyes,' Beth exclaimed.

'It must be a Highland cow,' said Granny, 'look at its mother's huge horns.'

At last the car turned up the long tree lined drive, past the paddocks and stables, over the little stream at the bottom of the garden and through the rhododendrons where the girls had made a camp.

Then the house came into view. Its soft grey stone walls were mellow in the evening light, and the windows twinkled in the last of the sun's rays. It had a steep slate roof and curly tall chimneys and sat in the middle of a neat lawn, surrounded by rhododendron bushes and trees. The girls loved its corners and oddly shaped rooms, with little steps up and down in unexpected places.

'Look, Minou is sitting on our bedroom window sill,' Beth shouted, waving wildly at the black and white cat who gazed calmly back.

Grandpa and Aunty Anna came out as the children

rushed around hugging everyone including Charlie dog and Minou (until she removed herself from the hurly burly), all talking at once.

2

Beth woke with the sun shining onto her face through a gap in the curtains. She could hear Anna moving around in the next room and slipped quietly out of bed.

'Can I come with you to feed the horses?' she whispered through the crack in her aunt's open door.

'OK. You'll need your welly boots, the grass is wet with dew.'

Beth burrowed in her bag for a T shirt and her old johds. They set off across the garden to the paddock with Charlie the Border Collie sniffing the scents left overnight by the woodland animals. The dew sent little wisps of steam into the air as the warmth of the sun dried the grass and the birds sang in the trees.

'I love early mornings here; it's so quiet you can hear the whole world breathing and there's just so much space,' Beth happily sighed spinning round and round, spreading her arms wide as she danced, smiling at her aunt.

'It's going to be a lovely warm day,' Anna said. 'Will you open the field gate while I make up the buckets of feed. Be careful to stand clear when the horses come into the yard as they tend to rush.'

Once she had the buckets ready she asked, 'Are they all in their stables now? The blue bucket with pony nuts and carrots is Bracken's; he's boss so he has his first. Summer's bucket is the yellow one. Tell her very firmly to go back. She has to wait until you've put down the bucket. Well done, Beth, you are getting brave,' Anna said as Beth pushed the big horse out of the way with her elbow, making her wait her turn.

'Now Magic can have her purple bucket,' she added, smiling.

'Isn't she patient, waiting till last. Oh, wow, listen, she said thank you,' Beth was thrilled as the little grey mare whickered gently before digging her nose greedily into her breakfast.

While the horses were busy eating, Anna and Beth swept up last night's hay from the ground.

'Just check the water trough is full while I collect the droppings in the field. Then we'll put their fly rugs on to protect them from the midges.'

'I think I can reach to put on Magic's rug, but I don't know if I can manage Bracken's.'

'That's fine,' Anna replied 'I'll do the other two. Remember to put her fly mask on her head to stop her eyes and ears being bitten.'

'Now they can go back into their field to doze in the sun,' said Beth giving Magic a last hug.

Beth and Charlie dog ran circles around each other across the lawn as they went back for their own breakfast. Niki and Lolly were already at the kitchen table tucking into bowls of cereal and there was the smell of toast in the air. As Granny poured juice for Beth, Minou jumped up onto her lap, purring loudly and rubbing her head on Beth's arm.

'That's a rather large mouthful Lolly – can you say "Puss"?' Granny exclaimed as Lolly rushed to finish her breakfast.

'Puff,' Lolly sprayed cereals over the table as she tried to say "puss", then made a face, her eyes wide with dismay. Niki and Beth giggled apprehensively, hoping Granny wouldn't be cross, but she just sighed, hiding her smile.

'The ponies need time to digest their breakfasts

before being ridden, so perhaps you'd like to go visiting first,' Granny said, as she cleared the table.

Chairs were scraped back over the tiled floor and Niki led the charge for the door, calling,

'Come on Charlie dog.'

'Where first?'

'Mrs Ambridge and Mrs Mavis?' Beth suggested.

'No, we'll keep them till later so they'll give us milk and biscuits,' Niki was used to bossing her sisters but did it quite nicely. She looked around thoughtfully.

'I know; let's check our camp is still there.'

They dived straight into the rhododendron bushes to search for their den.

'Oh good!' exclaimed Niki, 'The old tarpaulin roof we put up at Easter when it rained so much is still here.'

'The chairs and tables look very grubby,' said Beth, looking at the upturned logs and milk crates which furnished their camp. Beth loved the den and would happily potter around all day on her own. 'Can you reach the cupboard hanging from that branch, Lolly, and see if the tea set is still in there?'

Lolly climbed onto a crate and swept bits of leaves out of the metal cupboard.

'We'll borrow a brush from Granny and a washing up bowl and soon have everything spic and span,' said home maker Beth.

"Let's ask for some biscuits and orange juice as well," Lolly said, who, like Winnie the Pooh, always had room for a little something.

'We'll sort it later,' Niki said. She didn't want to waste their first morning cleaning.

'Shall we visit Mervyn in his workshop now?' asked Beth.

'OK, then it'll be time to visit the old ladies. They're bound to have a snack ready for us,' Niki said, who was getting hungry again herself. 'OK, next stop the forge.'

Mervyn the blacksmith lived in a cottage the other side of the drive. The girls pushed through a hole in the hedge.

'Ouch, bum, we'll have to make that hole bigger; it's filled in since last hols,' Niki groaned.

'Either that or we've grown,' Beth answered.

Lolly, holding onto Charlie's collar, led the way to the forge door.

'Good morning, Mervyn,' they shouted over the noise of the furnace. The blacksmith held out a grimy hand to each in turn; he even shook Charlie's paw.

'Hello my dears,' he said in his soft Hampshire accent. His deeply tanned face was weather beaten and his hands were horny and hard from his work. Wild bushy eyebrows made him look fierce but he had twinkling blue eyes and smiled easily.

'You here for long then? Do ye want yon ponies' hooves seeing to?'

'We don't know yet,' Niki answered importantly, 'but we'll check their shoes when we groom them later.'

'Well,' Mervyn replied, 'your aunty's bringing Summer in later today because she wants stud holes for a competition this weekend, so if the ponies want doing, you bring them along too.'

'What are stump poles?' Lolly asked.

'Stud holes, dummy,' Niki said impatiently. 'Studs in the horses' shoes stop them from slipping, just like spikes in football boots.'

Mervyn told Charlie to sit outside the forge so his coat wouldn't be burnt by sparks and then he showed the girls the wrought iron gates he was making for their grandparents.

'Looky here, I'll be putting some leaves and horse-shoes on the gates as decorations,' he said, letting them pick up the carved metal objects. 'They're all ready to be welded to the frames. Would you like me to put your names on the gates too?'

To a chorus of 'oh yes please, that would be so wicked,' he found a scrap of paper and an old pencil and Beth carefully printed out their names.

'You should have written Laura not Lolly,' Niki said looking over her shoulder.

14

'But no one will know who that is. No one ever calls me by my proper name, except my teacher when I'm naughty,' Lolly butted in. Sometimes even she had trouble remembering it.

'It must be time for elevenses by now. Let's go and see Mrs Ambridge.'

'Bye Mervyn; see you later,' the girls waved as they left.

Mrs Ambridge and Mrs Mavis lived behind their grandparents in a pretty house which had started life as two tiny cottages that seemed to lean against each other. They were waiting for the sisters in the kitchen, with three glasses of cold milk and a plate of chocolate biscuits already on the table. There was even a bowl full of water on the floor for Charlie.

'Hello girls, here you are again. My, how you've grown,' the old ladies exclaimed in chorus.

Mrs Mavis was very short with a round face and smiling mouth. Her white hair was tightly curled, and she wore a pretty blue dress that matched her eyes. She bustled around hugging the children and sitting them down. Mrs Ambridge was tall and thin with wispy hair pulled back into a flat bun. She loved her garden and, as usual, she was wearing the old corduroy trousers and checked shirt that she worked in. She had kicked off her welly boots and was paddling around the kitchen in a pair of ancient woollen socks with holes in the toes.

'You sit down there and tell us all about school. We heard you arrive last night. Are you staying long?'

The girls sat at the table and between mouthfuls of biscuits and milk chatted happily to the two old ladies about their school work and the outings they had been on, how Granny had collected them and what they intended to do during their holiday.

The old ladies smiled and nodded as they listened to the children all talking at once, knowing they would manage to unravel it all later. Once the snacks were finished, Niki was eager to hurry on.

'We must go, the ponies'll be waiting for us by now. Thank you very much for the biscuits and we'll come and see you again soon,' she said shooing her sisters out as they called their goodbyes.

Back at Granny's they collected their riding hats and pulled on their jodhpur boots.

'My boot doesn't fit,' Beth cried sitting on the floor.

'Silly, you've picked up Lolly's. Here, this one is yours,' Niki said, chucking it to her as they all laughed.

Charlie dog led the way as they climbed the five-bar gate to the stable yard where Anna was already leading Summer in from the field to be groomed.

3

'Shall we bring in Bracken and Magic from the field?' Niki asked Anna.

'Yes please. Their headcollars are hanging up in the tack room.'

The girls went to catch the ponies, who, ever hopeful for titbits, came readily to their calls. Niki gave Lolly a leg-up to ride Magic bareback into the yard while Beth led her.

'Mervyn asked if the ponies need their shoes looked at,' Niki said importantly as she lifted Bracken's leg.

'Look at the shoes while you clean out their hooves so you can make the decision yourselves. They shouldn't be thin or worn so flat they can't grip the ground,' Anna answered.

Beth couldn't quite reach Magic's back with the saddle.

'Would you like me to help when I've finished tacking up Bracken?' Niki asked before saying 'Good boy,' as he helpfully lowered his head for the bridle. He had been Anna's first pony when she was 10, so she'd taught him this helpful trick.

'He's good about his bridle but he still puffs out his stomach when I try to do up the girth,' Niki added as she struggled to pull the straps tight.

'You'll need to check it again before you mount, otherwise you'll find yourself – and the saddle – under his tummy,' Anna warned her.

'I know you rode without the lead-rein last holiday but I'd better lead you to start with as Magic might be naughty,' Anna said to Beth as she climbed into Magic's saddle.

Lolly sat on the gate with Charlie at her feet; impatiently waiting her turn, while her sisters rode around the paddock. She hated being the youngest and ran as fast as Niki and shouted even louder; all the girls had been sitting on the ponies since they were babies and Lolly was determined to come off the lead rein this summer.

'Sit up straight and keep your heels down,' Anna

reminded them as it had been a whole term since they last rode, adding 'Are you happy for me to let go now, Beth?'

'Oh yes thank you. I'm very comfortable on Magic,' Beth beamed.

Bracken was feeling frisky with such a lightweight rider, and without warning broke into a lively canter, nearly unseating Niki.

'Yikes!' Niki's shriek of surprise startled Magic and suddenly Beth too was cantering around the field after Bracken.

'Uh-oh this could be trouble,' Anna said as she leaned on the gate next to Lolly, only relaxing when she saw the girls had recovered their balance.

'Bring the ponies back to trot and then walk over to me,' she called after they had cantered around the field a few times.

'You managed that very well girls,' Anna praised them as they walked their mounts towards the gate breathless and smiling.

'Now it's Lolly's turn. Do up your hat and we'll pop you on Bracken first as his stride is longer and more comfortable. Niki can run beside you. Do you remember how to hold the reins? Good girl, now sit up straight.' They walked around the field then Niki coaxed Bracken into a trot. Lolly managed to rise to the trot really well. She was a natural.

'Well ridden,' Beth and Anna clapped as Niki brought the pony back to the gate with his rider grinning widely.

'Phew I'm puffed. Your turn to lead, Beth,' Niki threw herself onto the ground. Anna helped Lolly onto Magic and Beth led her around the field.

'Ooh, she's very bouncy after Bracken,' Lolly was giggling and breathless by the time they slowed down.

'I can't run any more,' Beth gasped laughing, as she too collapsed, putting her arms round Charlie.

'That's OK, I'll ride Bracken and lead Magic,' Anna said hopping easily onto the bay pony.

'Gee up Magic, let's hope Bracken doesn't bomb off again.' Bracken tossed his head, bouncing sideways as they walked round the field.

'Please can we go faster?' Lolly asked.

'Trot on,' Anna said to Bracken. Lolly laughed with delight as Magic cantered to keep up with him.

'Look at me,' she called to her sisters. 'I'm going soooo fast.'

'What's the competition Mervyn said you're going to?' Niki asked Anna later as they took the bridles and saddles off the ponies and hung them on their special hooks in the tack room.

'It's called a One Day Event, because you ride all three stages in one day. First is a dressage test, then a round of show jumping against the clock, and finally a cross country course which is also timed. That's the most exciting part, as you gallop over natural jumps like hedges, logs and water, out in the open country. I need to practise the dressage and jumping this week at home. You can help me set out the arena if you like.'

'Oh yes, of course we'll help.'

Anna paced out a dressage arena, counting her strides to lay the arena markers the right distances apart.

'Why have the markers got letters on them?' Lolly asked.

'The letters tell the rider where they are in the test, so that everyone does it the same. You can remember the right order for the arena letters by saying All King Edward's Horses Can Make Big Fences.'

'Why? What does that mean?' Lolly asked.

'The first letters of those words tell you which order to put out the markers, so everyone reads the instructions in the same way.'

'Here, Niki, this is the test I have to ride on Sunday. Will you read it out to me while the others put the ponies in the yard out of my way? Hang up a full haynet for them to share, girls, to keep them happy.'

Beth sat on the gate with Niki who, feeling very important, read out the instructions. Lolly and Charlie played together in a warm hairy heap on the ground.

'Enter at A and trot down the centre line,' Niki called.

Anna trotted Summer in a straight line down the centre of the arena.

'Track right at C and circle at B,' Niki continued.

Anna trotted to the end of the arena and turned right. When she reached the B marker she turned into the arena, riding a circle. Niki continued to call out the moves and Summer cantered around the arena, circling and twisting, changing pace to walk and then canter again, until Anna could feel that she was supple and obedient. She finished with a lively trot down the centre line, halting squarely. Then Anna asked Summer to stand still while she saluted.

'Good girl,' she said patting the horse's hot neck.

'That was beautiful,' breathed Beth. 'I want to ride like that.'

'You have light hands and you sit straight in the saddle, so you're well on the way,' Anna answered.

'Now we'll set up the jumps.' The sisters had helped their aunt before so they knew what to do. Anna carried the heavy jump wings into position and Niki and Beth carried the poles between them.

'Careful Niki – you're walking too fast,' Beth nearly fell as she tried to keep up with Niki. Lolly carried the jump cups, getting them in a tangle and managing to drop them as she crossed the field.

'I need two cups at each wing so I can rest the poles on them,' Anna showed Lolly how to push the cups into the holes on the wings. 'Make sure the poles are level,' she added.

With everyone working together they soon had two jumps close together with the third one further away at an angle, so that Anna could ride over them from different directions, making it seem as though there were more than 3 jumps.

'I'll just do a few rounds before lunch,' Anna told them. 'Then this afternoon you can have another ride when I bring Summer back from the blacksmith. We'll leave the jumps up in the field for the rest of the week so you can use them too.'

'We won't have to jump that high will we?' Beth asked anxiously.

'Oh no, don't worry, they can be lowered easily for you,' Anna replied soothingly.

Summer loved to jump and cleared all the obstacles easily; sometimes leaping so high that Anna was nearly bounced out of the saddle.

'We'd better leave the ponies in the yard with some hay while we have lunch, otherwise they'll be impossible to catch this afternoon,' Anna told the girls.

'There's a children's show and gymkhana in a few weeks. Would you girls like to enter?' Granny said at lunch time.

'Oh, wicked, but what would we have to do?' Niki and Beth crowded around Anna who brought up the schedule on her laptop.

'Can I ride too?' asked Lolly jiggling up and down with excitement, 'Is there anything for me?' she asked.

Being only five, she couldn't read very well, but she peered at the computer over Anna's shoulder, breathing hard in her ear.

'There's a Lead-rein Jumping class for you, Lolly, with a Minimus Jumping class for Beth and Junior Jumping for Niki. Then there are Mounted Games races which are great fun. I'll teach you the games; you can practise in the field.'

'Cool, that sounds wicked,' Niki clapped her hands, then quickly stopped, remembering that she was nearly eleven and too cool to clap. She couldn't help beaming.

'We'll enter both the ponies in Best Turned Out. I'll show you how to plait their manes when I prepare Summer for my competition this weekend. That'll give you a couple of weeks to practise.'

'Oh and look, there's a Dog Agility class and Dog with the Waggiest Tail,' Beth chipped in.

'That'll be just right for you won't it, Charlie,' Lolly grinned at the dog, who was giving a fine demonstration, waving his long tail high in the air.

'What's agi - agil - ag-lity?' she asked.

'Agility is a sort of obstacle course for dogs,' Anna told her.

'We can put up some obstacles on the lawn for Charlie before we ride this afternoon,' she added, laughing as Lolly jumped up and down in excitement.

'Calm down, Lolly,' Beth tried to sit on her small sister but they just ended up rolling around on the floor, giggling.

'That's settled then. I'll fill in the entry form on the website, and pay the fees by credit card. There, all done. Now you'll have to practise lots to make sure you're ready.'

After lunch, Anna took Summer to the blacksmith's forge while the girls searched for old chairs and tarpaulins, bamboo sticks and an old table to make an obstacle course for Charlie on the lawn.

'Come on Charlie,' Lolly put him on the lead and tried to persuade him to crawl under the tarpaulin.

'Ouf, no, you're supposed to follow me, not lick my face,' she collapsed laughing with Charlie dog on top of her.

'Give him to me,' Beth said. 'I bet I can make him behave. SIT. STAY.'

Charlie sat, looking rather surprised, then Beth crawled under the tarpaulin, pulling him behind her. He wasn't keen at first, but with Lolly pushing and Beth tugging, he managed to go through after a few attempts, crawling on his tummy. Then they stuck the bamboos into the lawn for him to weave between them.

'Come on Charlie, follow me,' Beth encouraged him, but being a big dog, he found weaving through the poles rather difficult.

'When Anna comes back, we'll take him into the field to practise over the horse jumps,' Niki said. 'but I don't know how we'll make a see-saw for him to walk over. Perhaps Grandpa will have some good ideas.'

'How about using a long plank of wood resting on two chairs with their legs tied together so the plank doesn't fall off,' Grandpa said. This worked quite well although Charlie preferred to jump on and off rather than walk along it, especially if he could leap off onto one of the girls.

'He thinks pushing us over and licking us to death is part of dog agility,' Beth gasped as he tumbled her to the ground yet again.

'We need to collect things for the gymkhana games too,' Niki said, organising her sisters.

'Anna said we'll need poles to stick in the ground for the bending race. Beth, go and ask Grandpa what we can use.' Beth sped away in the direction of the shed where Grandpa was working.

'Lolly, ask Granny for metal or plastic mugs and

some socks while I make some flags out of bamboo sticks and handkerchiefs.'

The girls rushed around begging items from Granny and Grandpa. Then when Anna came back from the blacksmith, she showed them how to set up the equipment for the races.

'We'll start with bending,' she said, mounting Bracken and trotting him down the line of poles, weaving in and out, turning at the end before cantering back.

'Stay in trot for now, you can work up to canter when you're confident,' she said helping Beth up onto Magic.

Niki and Beth rode both ponies down the line of poles, bending in and out until they reached the final post when they turned and came back up the line. Then Lolly mounted Magic and Anna led her through the poles. After that they all took turns at the mug, sock and flag races.

'In the mug race you just take one mug off the top of the first pole and put it on the fourth post; then you do the same with the others, moving the mugs from one pole to another,' Anna explained.

'Sock is more difficult. You ride to the end where a rolled-up sock is on the ground, jump off, pick up the sock, get back on and ride to the bucket in the middle of the course. Drop the sock into the bucket and ride to the finish.'

'The flag race needs a steady eye and a firm hand. You ride to the end and take a flag out of the cone, then you put it into the empty cone on your way back to the finish. Don't worry about getting muddled and dropping the equipment; the ponies know what to do and will help you,' Anna called out just as Niki fell off.

Then Magic stood on Beth's foot when she jumped off to pick up her sock.

'Oww that hurts,' Beth hopped around. 'Clumsy Magic, I can't get back on with you standing on my foot, silly.'

After several goes at each race, Lolly got cross when Magic, who wanted her tea, dug in her toes and refused to move.

'I think we've done enough for one day,' Anna said. 'Niki can help me with the ponies while you two collect the equipment and put it in the tack room ready for tomorrow. Then the ponies can have their supper before going out for the night.'

'Goodnight Bracken, goodnight Magic.' All three girls kissed and petted their favourite, and Anna lifted Lolly up to say 'goodnight' to Summer, who tossed her head and pranced off with her tail in the air.

'Supper's ready,' Granny called 'hurry up – it's spaghetti bolognaise.'

'Hurrah – WORMS – our favourite,' Beth and Niki shouted as they ran with Charlie to the house.

'Pag-sgetti,' murmured Lolly tiredly, holding Anna's hand as they followed more slowly.

4

The next few days were spent helping Anna to practise Summer's flatwork and jumping.

'What's flatwork, Aunty Anna?' Lolly asked.

'It's the exercises which make your horse supple and obedient, so he does what you ask. It's very important that they obey their rider calmly and promptly as otherwise it would be dangerous when you ride across open country.'

'Why would it be dangerous?'

'Because although the rider has walked the course, the horse hasn't, so doesn't know where to go or what is round each corner. The horse needs to trust his rider so they don't both come a cropper,' Anna answered.

For the rest of the week, the girls practised their gymkhana games on the two ponies, as well as giving the horses their breakfasts every morning, 'mucking out' the field and helping Anna keep the yard clean and tidy. They liked helping anyway but Anna had promised to buy them ice creams after her competition. Niki happily sat on the gate watching Anna ride Summer in the arena, practising the different moves; flying changes were always exciting to watch as well as ride, as the big horse could be exuberant and throw in a buck or two which made everyone laugh.

'Ooh, she's crossing her legs over – I hope she won't get in a tangle and fall over,' exclaimed Beth.

'That's a half-pass – she's supposed to cross her legs,' Niki said importantly.

'Now she looks as though she's hinged in the middle,' Lolly giggled.

'That move is called shoulder in, then going backwards is rein back,' Niki continued, in teaching mode.

'Jumping jellybeans. Now she's bucking. Poor Anna. Summer isn't being a good girl now.' The girls laughed, cheering as Anna grabbed her mane to help her hang on as Summer cracked her nostrils crossly.

'Dumb animal. What a ding-bat,' Anna exclaimed. 'Just canter and change leg when I ask you instead of bouncing around like a mad thing.'

Beth and Lolly didn't like sitting still for long, so

they took Charlie and played 'house' in the rhododen-drons, climbed trees or visited with the neighbours. If they were given biscuits they always saved some for Niki though they were usually a mess of crumbs by the time she found them.

When Anna had to go to work, Granny helped the sisters groom their ponies and practise the games.

'I'm trying to copy some of Summer's dressage moves on Bracken,' Niki told her. 'But he pretends he doesn't know what I want him to do.'

'Anna won plenty of dressage competitions on him when she was a girl. He's older now but he still knows what to do, so don't give up,' Granny said.

Niki took Granny's words to heart and rode Bracken around the arena again, even managing some half passes, as well as some rather lively bucks and prances.

'He can be very naughty,' she told Anna over supper, 'but I only fell off twice today so I must be getting better.'

They all enjoyed the games even though they col-lected plenty of bruises. Sometimes the ponies got over excited and bounced sideways or refused to stop. Beth was really quite happy to let Lolly have her turn as she often fell off when Magic turned quickly.

The little pony had to go slower when Granny led her, so Lolly always felt safe, even daring to jump off to pick up a sock before the pony had stopped. Lolly wasn't tall enough to mount on her own so Granny or Niki had to help her.

'Leg-ups are meant to be elegant but we don't seem to have got it right yet,' Niki collapsed on the ground giggling as Lolly scrambled grunting into the saddle while Magic stood, twitching her ears crossly.

At breakfast the day before her competition Anna gathered her troops.

'I need to bath Summer and plait her mane ready for tomorrow. As it's sunny, would you like to wash the other two so you know what to do before your show? We'll need shampoo, towels and buckets of hot water.'

Anna and Lolly led Summer and the ponies into the stable yard, while Niki and Beth struggled to carry three buckets of warm soapy water from the house.

'You'll need to stand on stools or the mounting block to reach to wash their manes.'

The girls watched while Anna carefully washed Summer's blaze and forelock with clean water so no soap went into her eyes, then they washed the ponies. Lolly thought Magic's long forelock which hung over her eyes was a bit like her own fringe, which did the same. When they had soaped and rinsed the tails, Anna showed the girls how to dry them by 'windmilling' Summer's, and they had great fun spraying each other.

The ponies were patient with all this attention. They had haynets to eat, and loved being petted and fussed over, but Summer was not a cuddly horse and restlessly threw her head around and stamped her hooves. She was very aware of her good looks and fidgeted, knowing she was being prepared for an exciting competition.

'Stand still, you monkey,' Anna exclaimed, skipping out of the way as Summer waved a hind leg in the air. 'You'd better behave tomorrow or I shall send you to the butchers,' she threatened the horse, laughing.

Anna showed the girls how to plait a mane, using a special comb to make 3 even bunches for each plait.

'Summer has a long neck so I make 11 plaits using this comb. You'll find that Bracken will need about 9, and Magic only 7.'

'Wow, Summer does look smart, especially with her forelock in a French plait,' Beth admired Anna's handiwork.

'I definitely need to practise some more,' said Niki as Bracken shook his head, making his plaits fly undone.

'I'll just put a light cotton rug on Summer to keep her clean and then we'll let them back out into the field.'

'Oh no, look at the ponies,' cried Lolly. 'They've found a dusty bit to roll in and now they've bits of grass sticking out of their manes and tails, and dust all over their clean coats.'

'Don't they look smug – and doesn't Summer look fed up that she can't get dirty too.' They laughed at her cross expression as she stalked across the field, driving the ponies before her.

'Instead of riding this afternoon, perhaps you'd help me clean the tack,' Anna suggested. 'Then we can load the car ready for an early start tomorrow.'

Niki, feeling very grown up, helped Anna while Lolly and Beth took Charlie onto the lawn where they gave him a bath so he too would look smart. Charlie quite liked being bathed but thought the best bit was when he could jump out of the bath and shake the water off his coat all over his friends.

'Help, I'm soaked through – Charlie stop it,' Beth shrieked. Lolly chased Charlie but he dashed off into the bushes.

'Oh no!' shouted Beth. 'Catch him Lolly!' But it was too late; he had found something sticky and smelly to roll in.

'We had to bath him again,' Beth explained to her grandparents over supper.

'Then he shook himself and we ended up having a bath too.'

'There's nothing so affectionate as a wet dog,' Grandpa said, laughing.

'Then we put on his lead and Beth ran up and down the dog obstacle course with him while his coat dried,' Lolly added.

'I'm afraid you two will have to have yet another bath after supper,' Granny said. 'But at least it'll be a hot one this time.'

The sisters curled up together on their big bed, plaiting each other's hair, while Grandpa sat in the comfy chair, reading stories and listening to their day's adventures. Lolly was asleep the minute her head touched the pillow and Beth was not far behind, but Niki lay awake daydreaming about riding Bracken in a competition and winning rosettes.

5

They were all up early the next morning. Anna and Granny fed the horses and hitched up the trailer to the Land Rover before breakfast. Granny kept remembering things to take and dashed around muttering under her breathe.

'Spare clothes in case it rains, both our mobile phones, Charlie's lead, Anna's second pair of boots in case the zip on her best pair breaks.'

'It happened once,' she told the girls, 'and Anna had to ride in borrowed boots that were far too big for her. Not easy and not safe either.'

Grandpa heaved a gusty sigh as he waved them goodbye in a whirlwind of excited chatter.

'After I've washed up, Minou,' he told the cat, 'I'll sit down with you and we'll watch sport on the TV until it's time to cook supper for them. We'd better make the most of today's peace and quiet as no doubt we'll be roped in again soon enough.'

Minou weaved around his legs purring and then sat on Grandpa's chair and washed daintily behind her ears until he had finished his chores. At the stables Anna issued instructions to her three helpers.

'Summer needs travelling boots to protect her legs from knocks in the trailer. Pass me her best lightweight rug, please Beth, and Niki, can you fill a large haynet? Lolly, you could put the grooming kit in the car.'

'Shall we make sure Bracken and Magic have plenty of water and turn them out in the field with their fly masks on?' Beth asked.

'That would be helpful,' Anna replied, 'Then I'll load Summer into the trailer.'

'I'll wait in the car with Charlie,' Lolly said, climbing into the Land Rover and talking to Charlie who was squashed in the back with the tack and picnic.

'Right, all aboard,' called Granny. 'Strap in everyone, and off we go.'

Anna was always quiet on the way to a competition, focusing on what she would have to do and checking that she knew the test. Granny drove carefully to ensure Summer had a smooth ride in the trailer, and the three girls played with their electronic games or talked quietly to each other and Charlie.

'No, Charlie, you can't get over the seat – stop licking me – ugh – Niki, get him off me.'

The New Forest looked enchanting in the early morning light, with its leafy glades and wooded areas. Ponies and cows grazed freely by the side of the road.

'I wish we lived here all the time,' Beth said. 'It's so beautiful.'

'Then we could have ponies of our very own...'

'and our own dog.'

'We'd have a beach hut,'

'and Grandpa could take us sailing.'

'Mmm. We'll have to work on Mummy and Daddy,' Niki decided.

At last they arrived at the show and were directed to the lorry park.

'Just open the top of the front ramp so Summer can look out while I go and get my number,' Anna said. Niki nodded, stretching up to unclip the top door.

'There you are, Summer, now you can watch the other horses and see where you are,' she said as the large horse looked out alertly at the hustle and bustle.

When Anna returned, she led Summer out of the trailer and took off her travelling boots and rug. Once she had tacked up her horse, she changed into white breeches, white shirt with a satin stock around her neck and her black jacket, hat and gloves. Her long hair was bundled neatly into a hairnet. She zipped up her long black boots and Granny made sure her number was tied firmly round her waist. Summer's coat shone in the sun. She tossed her head, arching her neatly plaited neck as she danced on her toes, waiting for Anna to mount.

'Why do you wear your hair tied back in that hair net?' asked Lolly.

'It keeps my hair out of my eyes and because it's tucked up, the judge can read the number on my back,' her aunt answered.

'You look so smart you should win Best Turned Out,' Beth was thrilled to see Anna looking so glamorous.

They followed Summer to the practice area before her dressage test. Anna found a corner where she could warm up quietly until it was her turn to enter the arena to perform her test. Granny tightened the horse's girth, and then ushered the girls closer so they had a good view. Charlie, who was an old hand at competition days, seemed to know what to expect and sat patiently watching. Summer bounced with excitement as she circled the arena, but Anna calmed her down as the judge rang her bell to signal that they should start. Both Niki and Beth were holding their breath as Summer trotted up the centre line.

'I've got my fingers crossed Summer behaves herself,' Beth whispered.

'Me too, it must be frightening knowing you have to get it right first time and everyone is looking at you,' Niki answered.

'That's a good straight entry,' Granny said.

The girls could hardly bear to breathe as the pair circled first in trot then in canter, crossing the arena diagonally and in serpentines, slowing again to a walk and then halting in front of the judge before Anna saluted. Serpentines were Beth's favourite; she loved how Anna made them look so graceful.

Summer jiggled a little as they finished the test, relaxing and stretching her neck while Anna patted her, smiling.

'That was like ballet on horseback,' breathed Beth entranced. 'Anna is so clever to be able to ride like that and Summer looked so beautiful.'

'Perhaps next year we can find you some junior competitions to enter on Magic,' Granny replied, with her arm around Beth's shoulders.

'That went well,' Granny said encouragingly as Anna joined them. 'You've really worked hard on her trot which has a good rhythm now.'

'She's much more settled these days, and her canter work is better, but she lost concentration towards the end and didn't want to stand still in front of the judge,'

43

was Anna's more critical response. 'All in all though, it's a good start to the day,' she admitted.

'Back to the trailer,' Granny called to Lolly who had wandered away with Charlie, 'and we'll have a sandwich and drink while Anna walks the show jumping course.'

'Can I come with you?' Niki asked Anna. 'I promise to keep quiet and not ask too many questions. Please…'

Anna smiled down at her earnest niece.

'Of course you can, but I must learn the course and work out how many strides to take between the jumps, so you'll have to be patient if I don't explain things straight away.'

Granny tethered Summer to the trailer, taking off the saddle and bridle so she could relax.

'Will you two set up the folding chairs and table from the boot? Bring out the cool box too; we might just have time for a quick drink.'

'Charlie looks thirsty, shall I give him a bowl of water, Granny?' Beth asked.

'You hold the other end of the rug, Lolly, then we can spread out the picnic for Granny.' Beth added; she liked being in charge when Niki was not around.

A different saddle and bridle were needed for jumping as well as boots to protect Summer's legs if she knocked a pole, but Anna didn't need to change her own clothes. She put studs into the special holes in the shoes which the blacksmith had made.

'What are those for?' asked Beth.

'These stop her slipping around the corners between the jumps,' Anna said, checking the final adjustments and then having a quick drink of water.

'Oh, yes, I remember now; Mervyn told us.'

'Lolly, please fetch the portable mounting block from the trailer locker,' Anna added, then climbed lightly into the saddle and headed for the next stage of the competition. Charlie was happy lying in the shade under the Land Rover so they left him tied securely to the tow bar with his bowl of water nearby.

'We'll let him rest now as he gets very hot in the sun, but he'll enjoy walking the cross country course with you later,' Granny told them.

'Off we go!' cried Lolly skipping along behind Summer. 'To the jumping.'

6

'I'll just pop over a few practice jumps before my round,' Anna joined the other riders in the warm up arena, where they were waiting their turn to jump.

'When we walked the course,' Niki explained importantly to her sisters, 'Anna measured the distances between the jumps so she knows how many strides Summer will take. She checked how far into the corners she has to ride so they come at a jump straight, and she worked out how fast she needs to go to be inside the time.'

'How does she know which jump to go over next?' asked Lolly.

'The jumps have numbers on them, and there's a

timing machine which starts when you cross its line before the first jump and then turns itself off after the last one,' Niki told her. 'There are penalties for jumps knocked down, or if the horse refuses, or they take too long to finish.'

'Well remembered, Niki. You'll find all that information useful at your show in a few weeks' time,' Granny commented.

'It sounds very complicated,' Beth sounded worried.

They watched a beautiful pure white horse with a pretty head, flowing mane and long tail that looked a lot like little Magic, and Beth dreamed of riding her own pony at just such an event.

'Let's sit on those straw bales by the arena,' Granny said. 'We'll be able to see all the show jumps from there.'

They watched several riders and horses who went before Anna; some knocked down a pole or two, and one rider fell off when her horse stopped in front of a jump.

'Uh oh,' Beth said giggling quietly. 'I thought she might manage to wriggle back into the saddle until the horse put its head down to eat the grass.'

'Mmm,' said Granny, 'some horses carefully keep their heads up to help their rider, but some are not so kind; perhaps that one doesn't really like jumping.'

48

At last it was Anna's turn; Summer trotted into the arena looking alertly at the jumps.

'She's the most beautiful horse in the whole world,' Lolly said bouncing up and down excitedly.

'Shush,' Granny gently calmed her. 'But of course, everyone thinks their own horse is best.'

The bell rang to tell Anna to start, and she put Summer into a bouncy canter and headed for the first obstacle. Summer loved jumping and flew over it much higher than necessary, making Anna work hard to steady her before the second jump. Then they settled into a steady rhythm. Summer knocked a narrow jump just after a corner which made the spectators gasp, but although it wobbled, the pole did not fall and they galloped towards the last jump which Summer cleared in grand style. Anna rode out of the arena smiling and patting her horse.

'Well done ... that was great ... isn't she clever ... good horse ... gosh wasn't she fast,' the girls all spoke together, crowding around. Granny gently pulled Lolly away from Summer who was very pleased with herself and still bouncing around. Everyone was smiling and talking at once as they made their way back to the trailer.

'That's a good job done,' Granny said to her daughter. 'Although you took a chance with that last jump.'

'I know,' answered Anna. 'But I didn't dare fight her

so just encouraged her to lift over it. She's ready to move up to the next height really, which might help her settle earlier.'

'Lolly will you stay and look after Summer with me while Anna walks the cross country course? then Niki and Beth can go too,' Granny said.

'Can we take Charlie with us please, Granny?'

'Yes, Beth, but you girls need to remember horses will be galloping past so keep a sharp look-out to make sure you don't get mown down. The judges at each fence blow a whistle when a horse is coming, so if you hear one, look around to find a safe place to stand out of the way.'

'Best not to hide behind any bushes otherwise you could startle a horse when it finally sees you,' Anna added as she changed into her trainers so she could walk quickly. 'Come on girls, I need to get a move on. I'll explain things as we go.'

Lolly found Summer's headcollar and poured some water into a bucket for her to drink. Granny removed the tack to sponge her down where she had sweated during the jumping. This time Summer wasn't interested in her haynet, she knew what was coming next.

'Look Granny, Summer's watching Anna walking out to the big fields where the horses are galloping up and down over the brown fences,' Lolly said.

'Yes, she always likes to know where Anna is. I'm

not sure if she feels safer when Anna is with her, or if she's just checking out the other horses,' Granny replied.

'We've time for a cup of tea for me and a juice for you,' she added, rummaging in the picnic bag.

'Can we have biscuits too, please? I'm really hungry now.'

'OK, it'll probably be another couple of hours before we can eat again. Then when your sisters come back, you and I can go to the secretary's tent to look at the scores so far.'

Anna returned alone.

'I left the girls near the water jump, watching the action. We saw a couple of riders fall off and one horse leapt into the water so hard I am sure it had its eyes shut. The rider certainly did. A great wall of water splashed up and soaked the judges!'

'Just like Bracken when you used to compete him,' Granny retorted. 'Now, if you can manage for a few moments, we'll go and look at the dressage scores.'

Anna checked her watch.

'I don't have to mount for another 30 minutes so there's time if you go now. I'll just sit and have a drink and a sandwich before tacking up again.'

Granny and Lolly made their way past stalls that were selling everything from expensive saddles to mugs and scarves, past the hot dog van and the photographers' tent, until they reached the secretary's caravan. There was quite a crowd in front of the score boards, but eventually they found themselves in front of Class 4 Sections A and B, and there was Anna's name, half way down Section B.

'Summer's class has been split into 2 as there were so many entries,' Granny said. Lolly spelt out the letters 'a n n a' when Granny pointed to her name, and then burst into tears.

'Whatever's the matter, Lolly?' Granny knelt by the sobbing girl with her arm around her shoulder.

'Everyone else has more marks than Anna,' cried Lolly. 'She's last and she looked so beautiful. She can't be last. She can't.'

Granny led her away from the crowd and hugged Lolly,

'It's all right poppet, honestly. At a One Day Event, it's the fewest number of points that wins. Anna's doing well at the moment. Her dressage score is good and she went clear in the jumping so there are no penalties to add. If the horses with better dressage marks have jumping or time faults, then she will overtake them.'

Lolly cheered up but was still hiccuping as they returned to the trailer, so Granny said,

'Listen, we'll just tell Anna she has a good score of 29 for her dressage but don't give her details. You see, once at a competition someone told her she was winning, and when we went to the prize giving we found they were wrong.'

'Oh, poor Aunty Anna, she must have been so sad.'

'So now I only say she's doing well because it is more important to try your best and enjoy yourself than worry about winning.'

Anna had already changed into her cross country clothes; a thick white linen stock around her neck instead of the lightweight satin one, and a white rugby-style shirt under her body protector.

'Do you need water wings if you fall off in the water?' asked Lolly, making Granny and Anna laugh.

'I don't, but perhaps Summer should have some,' was her reply.

Summer was keen to go, impatiently stamping her feet and tossing her head as Anna swung into the saddle. They set off for the start of the course, jogging sideways with excitement.

'We'll watch the start from the top of the hill then try to reach the water before you,' Granny called as they hurried after her.

'Good luck, take care, enjoy yourselves,' she added as Anna raised her hand, waving to let them know she had heard.

7

From the top of the hill they had a good view of the first four jumps on the course and could see horses cantering around waiting to start. Each horse in turn entered the start box while the starter counted down the seconds before telling them to go. Most set off steadily at trot or canter and jumped the first few jumps without problems, but some horses were over excited and wouldn't stand still.

One, having entered the start box, refused to come out and had to be coaxed towards the first jump, which he refused to even go near. After several attempts his rider gave in and headed for the second jump where the same thing happened.

'Why's that horse being so naughty, Granny?'

'It's probably a young horse who doesn't quite know what to do, but I expect she'll be allowed to carry on even though she's missed out some jumps. She'll have to keep out of the way of the other riders, then try to follow them to give her horse confidence,' Granny told Lolly.

'Oh look, it's Anna's turn,' Granny and Lolly held hands tightly. Even Granny was holding her breath as they watched Anna trot around the start box as the starter counted down –

3 . . . she entered the box . . .

2 . . . she pointed Summer's head towards the first jump . . .

1 . . . Anna leant forward in the saddle . . .

GO . . . and they were straight into canter. Granny breathed out again and Lolly bounced up and down giving a running commentary.

'She's over the first one, now she's over the second, oh what a big jump, she's coming, she's coming . . .' the pair thundered up the hill towards them, Anna's face fierce with concentration and Summer's ears pricked towards the next obstacle.

'Shh, quiet now,' murmured Granny softly, 'if they hear our voices it might distract them.'

At the top of the hill Summer cleared a big tree trunk and galloped into the next field where there were lots more jumps. Lolly and Granny ran down towards the lake where Niki, who had been listening to the commentator announcing each starter, saw them coming and waved.

'We're over here Granny.'

Beth had been lying down, dozing in the sun with Charlie as her pillow, but she sat up when she heard the loudspeaker reporting on Anna's progress.

'Anna Elliot riding Summer has cleared jumps 5 and 6 and they are powering towards the chair at 7. We have two riders on the course now and Summer is over the log at 8 and heading towards 9; number 10 is the water...'

'Here they come, here they are...' Beth was wide-awake and holding tightly to Charlie's collar as Anna and Summer galloped through an open gateway between two fields, heading towards the big log and into the water. Anna slowed the horse to give her time to see that they would land in water, then jumped cleanly over it sending spray into the air. They powered through the shallow lake and jumped up the step on the way out before galloping up the hill towards the next fence.

Niki shouted 'Jumping jellybeans! Did you see that – did you feel that – did you hear that? The ground shook, the thudding hooves; Summer's hot breath snorting and the water sprayed high and – oh, I want to do that, Granny, I want to gallop and jump!'

'It takes courage, but if you're brave enough there's no reason why you shouldn't.'

'I'm brave, I'm going to do that too,' Lolly stated loudly.

They ran, puffing, up the hill as they spoke. Anna had already finished and was walking Summer around to cool her whilst she waited for them.

'The commentator said you went clear,' Beth danced around. 'Gosh she is fast, isn't she? You looked fantastic. That was so exciting.'

'Niki, please hang up the saddle and bridle for me while I wash Summer to help her cool off.'

'I'll pour water into the bucket for you,' Beth offered.

'I'll put the wet boots into a bag,' Lolly picked them up and stowed them in the back of the car.

Anna made sure Summer was comfortable before she changed out of her own damp clothes.

'Let's sit and have the rest of the picnic – Anna is bound to be hungry by now. Would you top up Charlie's water bowl,' Granny said to Beth.

Summer looked very pleased with herself now she had calmed down; she knew she had finished and arched her neck, stretching her legs one at a time before letting Anna take the studs out of her shoes and put on her rug, then she tucked greedily into her haynet.

Once she had made sure her horse was happy, Anna sat down, enjoying a long drink of water before lying back on the rug as she told her enthralled nieces all about the ride.

'I saw the horse before us refuse to go so I kept Summer away from the start box until it was nearly time.'

'So she didn't have to stand and wait?'

'Yes, that's right, Niki. Because we were already trotting it was easy to go into canter and hold her steady for the first jump. She didn't really settle until the top of the hill, but then all I had to do was point her towards the next jump and she did the rest.'

'Did you see us at the lake?'

'Yes, Beth – I hope you didn't get too wet. She galloped up the hill after it like the wind. She was steady down the final slope so didn't miss the sharp turn to the last fences. She took on the "hole in the hedge" jump, even though it arched high above our heads. She was such a good girl. We had great fun,' Anna sighed happily.

'Quite a few horses stopped at the water jump,' Niki said. 'and some didn't like the hill after it.'

'The horses have to be very fit – the riders do too,' Granny explained. 'If the rider is tired half way round then they won't have the energy to control the horse and then the horse tires more quickly too.'

Anna jumped up suddenly; 'Right, who's coming with me to check the scores?'

'Me, me,' Niki walked beside her aunt and Beth skipped along too.

'Can I stay with you and the animals?' Lolly asked, cuddling up to Granny. She didn't want to look at the scores again. Charlie had gone to sleep and Summer was also dozing, resting her chin on the haynet with her eyes half closed. Lolly felt a bit sleepy herself now.

'Speak quietly when we go in to look at the scores,' Anna told the two girls 'it's not polite to make comments that other people can hear. I know I did quite well in the dressage but I need to see if I had time faults on the cross country course.'

'Oh, I don't think you could have,' Niki said. 'You were really fast; much faster than some of the others. Granny hardly had time to get to the water jump before you.'

'Unfortunately you can be marked down for going too fast as well as going too slowly; and Summer does like to set a good pace!' Anna answered, laughing.

Not everyone had completed the cross country so not all the marks were up, but Anna could see that her total points meant she would come at least third, depending whether the last few riders went clear. Two had better dressage scores than hers, but one already had 4 faults in the show jumping which left her only 1 point ahead of Anna.

'If this rider has any penalties across country, I'll move up into second place,' Anna said quietly, pointing at the board.

'What about the last one to go?' Niki pointed to the bottom of the score board where the final name only had dressage marks.

'He'll need to add 5 penalty points over the two jumping phases to make a difference to me. We'll have to wait until the prize giving before I'll know my final placing. Hopefully it won't take too long,' was Anna's comment. 'Let's go and look at the trade stands while we wait for the results. We'll take ice creams back for Granny and Lolly too.'

Niki and Beth had some pocket money so were happy to wander around the stalls. Beth was delighted to find a colourful velvet brow band with dainty rosettes on it.

'Magic would look so pretty in that,' she said, showing it to Anna, who agreed it would be smart in the Best Turned Out class at the children's show.

'Shall I buy these coloured leg wraps for Bracken?' Niki asked Anna.

'He doesn't really need them. How about this black whip instead?'

'I don't like whips. But this gold tie pin with a horse head looks smart.'

'What a good idea. It'll be useful and remind you of today every time you wear it,' Anna answered, as she rummaged through a bucket of odds and ends.

'Look at this pair of jodhpur boots – they've been reduced because they're a little scuffed. I reckon they're just Lolly's size,' she exclaimed holding them up.

'What a great find. Lolly will love having something new instead of hand-me downs,' Niki and Beth agreed.

They bought ice creams and made their way back to the trailer just in time to hear over the tannoy that the Prize Giving for Class 4, sections A and B would be outside the Secretary's Tent in 10 minutes.

'Heavens, that was quick. Here's your jacket and hat, Anna. Let me hold your ice cream while you put them on. Girls, wipe your faces so we look presentable,' Granny rushed round tidying up her family.

'Looking neat and tidy is a polite way of saying thank you to the organisers, especially if there are reporters taking photographs.'

Summer was still dozing quietly and Charlie was happy lying in the shade, so after telling the animals to behave themselves, they all headed to the Secretary's tent.

'We clap everyone, girls, and if Anna gets a good place, you can cheer as well,' Granny said.

'I've got my fingers crossed for her.'

'Me too,' Niki and Beth held up their crossed fingers and Lolly tried to cross hers.

'Mine won't cross – I'll cross my arms and feet instead,' she said, trying not to fall over.

There was quite a crowd of people waiting for the results but Lolly and Beth managed to wriggle to the front. Niki, being a big girl (of ten and three quarters) stood proudly between Anna and Granny but could not help jiggling around nervously.

'I'll start with Class 4 Section A.' There was a buzz of excitement in the crowd as the official stood on the caravan steps to read out the names of the riders in the first eight places, starting with the eighth and ending with the winner. After each name the crowd clapped as the rider came forward to collect their prize. Beth and Lolly gasped as they saw the huge rosette for the winner, and Beth whispered 'I hope Anna gets one like that.'

'Now for Class 4 Section B.' The announcer turned to a new page.

'This is Anna's class.' Beth hugged Lolly to keep her still. 'Quiet, ssshhh, listen."

8

As the names were read out the girls became more and more nervous. Anna had not been mentioned yet and already they were up to the fourth rider. She wasn't third either – the tension was desperate and Lolly felt tears roll down her cheeks as she tried not to make a sound when another name was called out for second place. Beth was digging her finger nails into her hands and all three girls (if truth be told probably Anna and Granny too) were holding their breath.

'And now the winner in Class 4 Section B is...'

'Oh, get on with it,' muttered Granny.

'...Miss Anna Elliot on Summer.'

The girls clapped and cheered, jumping up and

down hugging each other as Anna, grinning happily, pushed her way to the front and accepted the large scarlet rosette with its brightly coloured streamers and the first prize – a smart stable rug for Summer.

The winners had their photographs taken for a national horse magazine, and then the photographer came back to the trailer with them for another of Anna with Summer.

'I'll take some of you youngsters as well, if you like,' he suggested. 'I'll put them on the website so you'll have a record of today.'

'Can we borrow your mobile to ring Mummy and Dad to tell them we helped you win?' Niki asked Anna.

'I think I'll just have one last cup of tea while you load Summer and finish tidying everything away.' Granny sighed with relief that the day had been so successful and they could soon be on their way home.

Grandpa and Minou proudly produced supper when they arrived home.

'Fish and chips all round, with the compliments of the chef at our village chippy. Please note the elegant presentation in the paper wrappings,' Grandpa said with a flourish which made the girls giggle.

'How did you know when we'd be back, Grandpa?' asked Beth, picking up a chip in her fingers, adding 'Oww, that's really hot.'

'Anna texted me when you left so I knew when to expect you,' he replied.

'I hope you've bought mushy pea fritters too,' Granny said as she dished out the chips.

'Of course I did,' Grandpa was indignant. 'There's half a pea fritter each, and half a pineapple fritter each too. Now, sit down and tell me all about the competition.'

'We had a wonderful day and Anna won,' Beth said quietly, smiling up at Grandpa as she sneaked a piece of fish to Minou under the table.

'Yes, and so did Summer,' Lolly shouted. 'She loved galloping through the water.'

'It was so exciting, Grandpa. Summer danced and jumped and galloped and she and Anna won by miles. I'd love to ride across country like that one day,' Niki said.

'And I've got a new pair of johd boots,' Lolly said, waving her feet around to show them off.

At last supper was over and cleared away and every-one relaxed in front of the TV.

'What are we doing tomorrow Anna?' asked Niki, fighting a yawn.

'Nothing planned; let's wait and see how we feel in the morning,' Anna replied.

'Right; bedtime; quick bath then Grandpa will read

to you,' Granny said firmly. 'Look, Lolly's nearly asleep on the floor with Charlie.'

The next morning Granny asked, 'What would you like for breakfast Lolly; fleas' knees or flies eyebrows?'

'Umm, flies eyebrows please.'

Granny poured All Bran into a bowl and added some raisins, cranberries and milk. Lolly soon polished off her cereal while Minou, the cat, sat beside her watching every spoonful.

'All right Minou,' she said, 'I know you want to finish the milk.' She held the bowl out to the greedy cat.

The rest of the family came in yawning and stretching. Minou went from child to child begging for her share. Grandpa read his newspaper.

'Summer and I are going to have a well deserved day off after the excitements of yesterday, so if you like I'll give you proper lessons on the ponies today,' Anna offered. She enjoyed teaching her nieces.

'Oh yes please, that would be great; can we jump and do dressage?' Beth clasped her hands, while Lolly immediately rushed off to fetch her hat, shouting,

'Me first on Magic; it's my turn to ride first.'

'I need to practise the gymkhana games on Bracken,' Niki said. 'I can't always get back on quickly enough and he won't wait for me.'

The gymkhana games were hard work but caused

lots of laughter too. The girls soon stopped dropping the equipment and began to race the ponies against each other in the field. Anna led Magic at breakneck speed, with Lolly laughing delightedly as she grabbed mugs, jumped off to pick up socks, or caught flags and then stuck them into the top of a cone.

Bracken, remembering his youthful competition days with Anna, forgot his age and galloped round the poles, sliding to a stop and sometimes sending Niki over his head. She quickly learnt to hold on to his mane!

Magic refused to be outdone by Bracken and put her ears hard back, galloping as fast as she could to keep up. At first Beth wanted to stay in trot, but when Magic took it into her head to dash after Bracken she realised the speed was fun and didn't hurt – as long as they stopped together. Anna enjoyed the games just as much as the girls, and showed them how she used to vault onto Bracken.

'It's a long time since I tried this but here goes.'

She ran alongside Bracken, holding the reins and his mane as he cantered. Then she propelled herself up onto his back – and straight over the other side landing on her bottom!

'Are you hurt? Gosh that looks so difficult. Will you try again?' The girls couldn't help laughing. Anna pulled a face at them and tried again and this time vaulted into the saddle.

'Hooray! You did it. Well done,' her audience cheered and clapped.

Another attempt saw Anna miss again and Bracken galloped off at full speed with her still running alongside, making the girls shriek with laughter.

'Can we do some jumping now,' Niki called as Anna recovered with as much dignity as she could while Bracken stopped and smirked at her.

Anna laid out the poles on the ground for the ponies to trot over.

'Stand up in the saddle, chin up, hands down, heels down,' she called and the girls collapsed giggling in their saddles as they tried to maintain the "jumping position". Then Niki and Beth took it in turns to hold Lolly's lead rein but she was soon quite happy to take Magic herself as the pony never cantered off with her, although she did sometimes stop to eat the grass.

'You can't be hungry Magic. Get your head UP,' Lolly tried not to be cross as she hauled on the pony's reins.

'Oh well, I suppose it is time for lunch; let's turn the ponies out in the field, then we'll spend the afternoon on the beach.'

9

At supper Granny said, 'Grandpa and I have found a whole load of things we don't need any more which I'm taking to the Sunday car boot sale. It'll mean a very early start but I should be home by lunch time. If anyone would like to come and help they'll be most welcome. I expect there'll be some interesting things to buy too.'

'Oh yes, I'll come. I need to find presents for Mummy and Daddy.' Niki liked the idea of looking around the stalls.

'You can often find really good bargains and hopefully some new riding clothes which you all need for the show,' Granny added.

'Perhaps we'll find treasure, diamonds or jewels.' Lolly began bouncing at the thought.

'Mummy gave us some pocket money; can we take it with us?' asked Beth.

'I'll give the ponies their breakfast for you,' Anna said. 'Then I'm meeting my friend Emma for a long fast ride on the Forest as part of Summer's fitness programme. We're having a pub lunch at The Oak so I'll be out all day. You lot can ride on your own when you get back if you like.'

'Grandpa and I'll load the car tonight as it's an early start. We can buy bacon butties from the van at the sale field for breakfast, and we'll take drinks and nibbles to keep us going,' Granny said. 'Off for your baths now.'

It was just after six o'clock the next morning when Granny woke the sisters.

'Wrap up warmly, girls, it's cool this morning. We need to leave soon.'

With everyone strapped in and the picnic basket safely stowed under the girls' feet, Granny headed down the drive leaving a very sad looking Charlie in the kitchen. He stood up on his hind legs watching out of the window and whining.

'Sorry Charlie, you'll have to stay with Grandpa today,' Niki called.

'Poor Charlie,' cried Lolly 'can't we take him with us – he'd be very good.'

'He'd soon be bored. Don't worry, Grandpa will let him out into the garden once we've gone, and he'll take Charlie with him if he goes down to the boat,' Granny reassured her.

'See you this afternoon, ponies,' they called to Bracken and Magic as they passed the field.

Granny and Niki it didn't take long to erect the folding tables, while Beth enjoyed practising her artistic talents as she helped set out the items for sale.

'Bring the china over here, Lolly; we'll make it look as though the toys are having a picnic. Let's put them on the plastic sheet in front of the tables so that passing children can see them easily.'

Niki carefully laid out books and CDs while Granny displayed vases and bowls, tools, pictures and an assortment of knick knacks.

'Take some money from my purse for our breakfast from the catering van. Come straight back so the butties will still be hot and then you can take turns to look around the other stalls.'

'Mmm, don't they smell divine,' Beth sniffed the bacon. 'Oh, goody, you remembered the tomato sauce.'

Beth and Lolly soon grew bored with selling and happily skipped off to look at other people's items for sale.

73

'Especially look out for riding clothes; you all need proper jackets, ties and gloves for the pony show,' Granny called after them.

Soon they had collected quite a pile of goodies, ranging from books and puzzles to a money box, a large floppy sun hat for Mummy and Lolly had quickly fallen in love with a large cuddly dog which had a zip in its back for her pyjamas.

'Oh look, Lolly, a riding jacket – and it fits me. Please run and fetch Granny,' Beth said, rummaging through a clothes stall in the hope of finding more goodies.

'What luck; I noticed yours is a little small now,' Granny agreed.

'Now you can have my old one Lolly,' Beth said. 'It's still in good condition and will be just right for the show next week.'

Beth also found a green tie with horse heads on it, and a red one with stirrups and spurs. Lolly unearthed a bag full of ribbons and lace.

'We don't need the lace but those red ribbons will look great in your hair for Best Turned Out,' Granny decided. 'Keep on looking girls, we still need another tie – it can have stripes or spots. But NOT mice or cats,' she added as Lolly held up one with cartoon characters.

'Thank you for looking after my stall, Niki; would

you like to go goody-hunting now?' Granny praised her oldest granddaughter.

'I sold tons of stuff, Granny, and now I know how to bargain for things I want to buy.'

Niki worked her way around the car boot sale methodically, one aisle at a time. She quickly spotted a pink bicycle and asked if she could try it out.

'Just right for me,' she thought, 'and the basket on the front will be very useful.'

Lolly wanted a doll's push chair and added that to her pile.

'I'm not sure how we'll get it home but we'll worry about that later,' Granny said.

'Now I think it's time for a little something, before you girls buy more than we brought to sell.'

The girls were admiring Beth's new jacket when the young girl from a nearby stall came over.

'I have a couple of pairs of johds which should fit you,' she said, holding up 2 pairs of creamy yellow johds. Niki pounced with a cry of triumph.

'Oh,' she breathed, 'they're gorgeous, I hope they fit... can I try them on?'

She kicked off her shoes and immediately pulled on the larger pair over her shorts. Beth grabbed the other pair and turned to Lolly, saying 'These look just right for you, let me help.' as Lolly struggled to pull them on over her shoes. Once Niki and Lolly were wearing the johds, Beth put on her jacket and the three paraded in front of Granny.

'Don't you look smart,' she said. 'Oh, and what's that in the pocket Niki? Look, it's a red and white spotted tie which will match the hair ribbons. Now we just need to find you white shirts and you'll be all set for the show.'

At last their tables were almost empty so the sisters went for a final look around.

'We still need some white shirts; I'm sure I saw a couple at the bottom of a pile over here … yes, here they are; one's still in its wrapping, I expect someone bought the wrong size. How much are they?' Niki began to bargain with the stall holder.

Lolly ran over to Granny with the shirts. 'Look, Granny, look, aren't they great.'

Granny was delighted and gave Lolly a big hug.

'You've all been such a help,' she said. 'Let's pack up the car, and as a thank you for your hard work, we'll buy ice creams on our way home.'

10

'Granny, can we ride now? It doesn't look as if Anna's home yet so we won't have to worry about Summer getting in our way. We can sort out the things we bought later,' Niki had already planned the afternoon.

She and Beth rushed upstairs to change into their old johds and riding boots, while Granny and Lolly prepared for a trip to the village shops.

'I wish we'd found me a new pair of boots too,' Beth sighed as she tugged hers on. 'Mine are very scruffy now and the soles are coming away. They'll never last until the show.'

'P'rhaps Granny will know where to find some. Come on, let's ride our bikes to the field; we'll put a drink and our hats in my new basket,' Niki urged her sister to hurry.

Calling to the ponies, Niki and Beth held the head-collars behind their backs as they walked across the field and held out carrots to entice the ponies to come to them.

'Here Bracken, come on Magic. Lovely carrots.'

The ponies looked up from the grass, interested but wary. They weren't sure they wanted to be caught. Magic was tempted by the tasty carrot and allowed Beth to slip the rope round her neck before putting on the headcollar. Bracken was standing a little further away and on seeing his friend caught, he tossed up his head and trotted off with his tail in the air.

'Oh no,' Niki groaned. 'He wants to play. Bum.'

Sure enough, every time she got close, he tossed his head and pranced out of reach, trotting around her in a circle. Then he halted, allowing Niki to hope that this time he would give in. But no, off he went again. At last Niki, being only ten and three quarters, lost her temper and stamped her feet.

'You horrible pony; I hate you,' she shouted, throwing the headcollar onto the ground as she stormed off to the stable.

Beth quietly led Magic in, picking up the dropped headcollar on the way. Once Bracken had no one to play with he turned and cantered across the field, pushing past Magic into the yard where he nuzzled the crying Niki to show he was sorry. Niki flung her arms around his neck, sobbing gently into his mane and Beth, having tied up Magic, quickly put on Bracken's headcollar so he couldn't escape again.

'He is a tease, isn't he?' she said trying to comfort her big sister. 'Anna says he does it to her too. She chases him around the field on purpose sometimes and he loves it.'

'Do you remember seeing her play Grandmother's Footsteps with him?' Niki had stopped crying. 'She pretended to walk away from him and when he followed her, she would turn around and run towards him so he galloped off. Then she would creep up behind him and shout "boo" and they would run after each other again.'

Soon both girls were laughing as they happily groomed their ponies. Beth needed Niki's help to put on Magic's bridle and do up her girth. Niki had to stand on the mounting block to reach when putting on Bracken's saddle.

'I'm not sure their girths are tight enough, we'd both better use the mounting block. Do up your chin strap properly, Beth,' Niki was back to being bossy, but she was grateful to Beth for her sympathy and spoke gently.

The girls walked the ponies around the field side by side, just relaxing in the warm afternoon sun.

'Isn't this just fab, Beth,' Niki lay flat on Bracken's back, holding the reins loosely as they ambled along.

'I wish the ponies were really ours and we could take them home. But they would miss all their wild friends, the rabbits, badgers and foxes, and the buzzards in the sky...'

'If we had the ponies at home, I wouldn't even mind going to school,' her sister agreed.

The ponies were soon bored with walking and started jogging which quickly ended the girls' dreamy mood. As the bending poles were still up they raced each other a few times, and finally popped over a few small jumps.

'Bracken needs a walk to cool off. Shall we ride down the drive and back again?' Niki felt very confident and was keen to take the ponies out of the field. 'We might see Anna or Granny coming home.'

Niki dismounted to open the gate. Fortunately there was an upturned log to help her remount once they were through.

'Better check your girth before you get on again. You don't want the saddle to slip round,' Beth reminded her, giggling.

'Don't laugh; it wouldn't be funny,' Niki replied, but she giggled as well at the thought of ending up under Bracken's tummy.

They walked the ponies down the long drive, feeling

very grown up; then turned back before reaching the road and trotted up to the house to see if anyone had come home. All was quiet so they walked back down the drive again, just as Anna, with Summer in the trailer, turned in from the road. They waved, waiting on the grass as she passed, then trotted after her.

'My word, you do look confident on those ponies, both of you,' Anna said as she got out of the car and lowered the ramp. 'We had a really good ride too, didn't we Summer. She was quite fresh to start with and loved being out with her friend Smartie. They were both frisky so we had a good long canter and then they settled down.' Anna stroked her horse's nose as it rested on her shoulder.

While she cleaned Summer's legs, muddy from wading through some streams, Niki and Beth untacked Bracken and Magic and prepared their buckets for an early tea.

'We found new johds for Lolly and me and a smart jacket for Beth at the car boot sale.'

'And some red ribbons for our hair and horsey ties to match. Granny says we'll look the bee's knees at the show. But look Anna, the sole is flapping off my johd boot,' Beth held up her foot and waggled it about. 'Can it be mended?'

'Hmm, that's not good. Let me think about it,' Anna said wrinkling her nose.

'Come on girls,' she added 'let's leave Summer's

muddy boots out to air and finish tidying up tomorrow. The pub lunch Emma and I had was a long time ago and I'm hot and thirsty and looking forward to a relaxing bath. Would you like a lift back to the house?'

'No, we'll cycle back across the lawn, thanks.'

'Oh, my, that's a smart new bike. Did you buy that at the car boot sale too?'

'Yeah, Granny said we came back with more than we took.' Niki replied and they all laughed.

Niki and Beth sprawled on the lawn and were just tucking into chocolate spread sandwiches when Granny and Lolly returned from their shopping trip. The three girls sorted out their car boot buys on the grass while Granny went indoors to make a cup of tea.

'I'm glad we rode first. It's more fun opening our bags now, when we've forgotten what we bought this morning,' Niki said. Granny sat in a deck chair with her tea, joined by Anna who felt refreshed after her bath.

The girls helped Granny empty her bags and found the johds, jacket, ties and ribbons, which they shared out and added to their piles.

'At least I came home with slightly less rubbish than I sold,' Granny said laughing.

'I'm afraid Beth's riding boots are unsafe and she certainly can't wear them at the show,' Anna told Granny when the family sat down to supper.

'I'll phone the Pony Club and see if they have any for sale,' Granny decided. 'We can't have her tripping up or catching her feet. Thank goodness Niki has some new ones and you found that good pair for Lolly.'

As they ate they worked out a plan of action for the next few days.

'I have to work every afternoon next week,' Anna announced. 'So Summer can have a rest tomorrow and after that I'll ride in the mornings. You girls can ride in the afternoons, or go to the beach, if you like.'

'Then on Thursday we'll take them all out to the forest, so they don't get bored with games and jumping in the field,' she added.

'That's not fair. I won't have anyone to ride when we go to the forest!' Lolly shouted, near to tears. 'I need a pony of mine own instead of having to share.'

'Calm down; you don't think I'd leave you out. I asked my friend Emma today. She says she'll ride with us and bring her Shetland pony Fudge for you to ride.'

'Oh, wow, I've always wanted to ride in the New Forest with all the wild ponies and the open spaces. Can we gallop?' asked Niki.

'Knowing Bracken, I expect you will, whether you want to or not,' Anna replied, laughing at the girls' startled expressions. 'Don't worry Beth. I'll keep hold of Magic if you don't want to go that fast.'

'Yes, but Summer will want to gallop, and if you're holding me...' Beth said nervously.

'You'll be fine, Beth. Emma's horse is very quiet so I'm sure she'll look after you if Summer gets too bouncy,' Anna gave her niece a reassuring hug.

'Then on Friday the ponies must be bathed and plaited ready for the show, and Granny will wash all your riding clothes. We'll clean the tack until it gleams before you lot have a hair wash and bath, too.'

'Don't forget we have to bath Charlie as well,' Lolly spoke up.

'Yes and you still need to practise leading Charlie so he doesn't pull you over in the Waggiest Tail class. The Dog Agility is coming on well, Beth, but you still need to be firmer with him.'

Anna and Niki cleared away the plates while Granny dished up apple crumble and Beth passed round the custard.

'Well, that's next week organised – let's hope the weather holds. I think we should have a day just mooching around tomorrow, doing not much of anything in particular. A lazy day for everyone, although we might find the energy to wander down to the village for an ice cream later.'

11

They spent the next few days jumping and practising the gymkhana games.

'Magic has learnt the games really quickly,' Beth said, pleased and proud of her much loved pony.

'She races after Bracken just as fast as her little legs will carry her. The only problem is the stopping; sometimes it's so sudden she throws me over her head.'

A few minutes later Beth was struggling to her feet yet again, rubbing her bruised bottom.

'I know you need to get off in the sock race, but it's better to land on your feet, Beth, not in a heap,' Anna said, trying not to laugh.

'But what can I do? It's all right for Lolly, Magic

doesn't go as fast when you're leading her. Anyway, it's not so much the fast canter which makes me fall off; it's stopping so quickly I can't do.' Beth was trying hard not to cry.

'Oh dear, you have got some nasty bruises, haven't you, but you've been very brave,' Anna gave Beth a cuddle. 'Magic just wants to keep up with Bracken. You'll have to anticipate the end of the line. She'll respond to your voice so try saying "Whoa" as well as tugging on the reins a few strides before the end. Sit up straight, too, that might help. I'm sure she doesn't want you to keep falling off. How about giving it one more try, you're almost there.'

Anna gave Beth a leg up and started their race again.

'Watch the flag, wait for it to drop, then go,' Anna reminded them.

'The ponies are watching the flag too,' Lolly called, wriggling impatiently as she perched on the gate. This time, when it dropped the ponies set off almost without encouragement.

'SIT UP,' yelled Anna as they neared the end of the line of poles 'Talk to her, pull the reins.'

Beth sat up and shouted "whoa" and Magic slowed slightly before sliding to a stop just over the pile of socks.

'Way to go,' yelled Lolly falling right off the gate in her excitement. 'You did it Beth, you stayed on.'

A grinning Beth had jumped off the pony, collected her sock and remounted. Magic was very good and stood still until she felt Beth's leg across the saddle and then was off, back up the line of poles like a streak of lightning, with Beth still struggling to find her stirrup.

'At least we only have to dismount in one race,' Niki said as she hopped alongside the jiggling Bracken, with one foot in the stirrup as she tried to remount. 'And even though he won't stand still for me to get back on, his turns are really good in the flag and mug races.'

'Lolly's turn now on Magic. While I lead Lolly through the games, how about you pop Bracken over the jumps and then we'll lower them for Magic.'

Niki cantered Bracken over the jumps a few times, followed by Beth who ran with Charlie dog off the lead, encouraging him to jump over them too.

'We need to practise Dog Agility, Charlie. You'll have to learn to jump them on your own 'cos I can't keep up,' she puffed as they headed for the course.

'Come on Charlie, over the jump,' she called to him, jumping over herself. 'Now the next one OVER.' Every time she called OVER and he jumped she praised him, ruffling his fur and hugging him. At last she was able to just run towards a jump and shout OVER for Charlie to jump it by himself.

'I think he's nearly ready,' Beth said, dropping to the

ground. 'He loves it, and he never seems to get tired,' she added as he lay panting beside her.

Once she got her breath back, Beth took Magic over the jumps and then Anna led Lolly over them too.

'I think that's enough for now,' Anna said, 'I'll turn Summer out in the field while you girls untack the ponies, then I must have a shower before work. Will you lot tidy up the stable yard and tack room before lunch?'

'Charlie, come here!' Niki yelled suddenly, grabbing his collar so Summer didn't tread on him.

'Have a good afternoon on the beach,' Anna waved and dashed off to change.

Summer had watched from the stable yard and was delighted to be turned out in the field. With her head and tail held high in the air she trotted with floating strides to join Bracken and Magic. All three animals then pranced with pleasure at their freedom and galloped off to the end of the field before racing back.

'Ooh,' squealed Lolly 'they aren't going to stop...' but at the last minute Bracken turned and the mares followed him before galloping away again. Just for fun Summer flew over one of the little jumps as she ran. The girls watched wide eyed until the horses calmed down and began to graze.

'Gosh, I'm glad they've stopped belting around. That

was a bit TOO exciting without Aunty Anna here,'
Niki said, carefully checking that the field gate and
tack room were properly shut before they went in
for lunch.

12

The next day the weather for their forest ride was dry but cloudy.

'Good thing too,' Granny said at breakfast. 'Otherwise you'll be uncomfortably hot with flies pestering the horses. This breeze will keep them away.'

The girls were mounted and becoming impatient by the time Emma trotted up the drive on Smartie with a very hairy Shetland pony alongside. Anna smiled at her friend as they all waved in greeting.

'Lolly, come and say hello to Fudge. She's a typical Thelwell pony – all stomach and masses of hair. I hope your legs will reach around her.'

'Oh she looks lovely,' Lolly said, stroking the little pony's soft nose. 'What's a Thelwell pony?'

Anna smiled as she answered. 'Thelwell was an artist who liked to draw little girls on short fat ponies like Fudge – I'll put a couple of his books of cartoons in your bedroom for you to look at later if you like.'

Fudge's forelock was so long her bright eyes were mostly hidden and her mane sprouted wildly on both sides of her neck. Her tail even dragged on the ground. 'That's because her legs are so short,' Emma told them as the little pony peeped out from under her bushy forelock.

'She has the daintiest tiniest hooves I've ever seen,' Beth said happily.

Anna did up Lolly's hat carefully. 'Once you're sitting on Fudge I can adjust your stirrups so your legs are comfortable.'

Then she tightened everyone's girth straps and checked Niki and Beth's hats before mounting Summer, who pranced excitedly. Smartie stood quietly while Emma picked up Fudge's lead rein.

'Steady there Summer, have some patience,' Anna gathered up the reins, calming the horse with her voice. 'Pass me your lead rein please Beth,' she added. 'Out of the way Charlie. Everyone ready? OK, Wagons Roll.'

Anna led the way down the drive, along the

bridle-path until they reached the open forest, with Magic jogging along beside her, Bracken in the middle and Smartie walking slowly to allow little Fudge to keep up. The sisters were thrilled to be out in the open forest, riding along the sandy tracks and inching through the gorse bushes.

'Keep your knees in so you aren't pricked by the gorse,' Anna called.

'Ouch. It's all right for you,' grumbled Niki as Bracken passed between two prickly bushes. 'You can keep your legs above the gorse on your tall horses.'

'We'll trot across this open green,' Anna decided as Charlie bounded ahead of the horses and then raced back to them with his tongue hanging out.

'Look at Charlie – he's loving this,' Beth exclaimed, laughing as he circled the horses. 'I think he's trying to round us up.'

'Well, he is a sheep dog,' Anna replied.

Lolly found Fudge's short stride quite difficult in trot, so Emma asked Smartie to trot faster, making little Fudge tuck her chin into her chest and break into a gentle canter.

'That's better,' Lolly said as she cantered beside the trotting Smartie, 'no more trot for me.'

Bracken was keen to lead the way and pushed ahead of Summer. Niki was nervous at being in front.

'I don't know which way to go,' she called. Before

she knew it, Bracken had taken the bit between his teeth and with an excited buck, broke into a gallop.

'Help. I can't stop,' she yelled, hanging on grimly to Bracken's mane.

'Turn him. Just turn him towards us,' Anna shouted at the rapidly disappearing pair, trying to hold back Summer who was dancing sideways, keen to join in the fun.

'He'll stop if you turn circles,' she yelled again as Summer continued to prance, making Beth cling on to Magic, trying not to cry.

Bracken turned as he reached the end of the long green, allowing Niki to shorten her reins so she could circle him on the way back to the others.

'Jumping jellybeans, that was a bit TOO exciting,' Niki gasped, red faced and with streaming eyes, as Bracken skidded to a halt in front of his friends.

'Would you like to canter on your own Beth?' Anna asked.

'No, I don't want to go that fast,' Beth shook her head.

'Don't worry, you'll be fine. Magic will look after you. Just let me grab Bracken's rein so he doesn't follow you.' Anna undid Magic's lead rein and Beth nervously asked her pony to trot and then cantered ahead on her own.

'If Bracken had gone too, heavens only knows when

we would have seen you both again,' Anna explained to Niki. 'Now let's find some small bushes to jump. You go first Niki, then I'll take Summer over and Beth can follow me. I don't think Fudge has done any jumping, Lolly, so it's probably not wise to start out here.'

Anna watched Bracken head for a low gorse bush and reminded Niki to turn him back after the jump. Magic followed Summer, who thought it was quite small but VERY prickly and her extravagant leap made them all laugh.

As the girls grew more confident, they found plenty of bushes, small logs and ditches to jump; one log lay right across their path and Fudge, cantering beside Smartie, jumped it before anyone had time to think! After that Lolly was determined not to be left out. It was lucky that Smartie was a quieter horse than Summer so Emma was able to hold onto the lead rein as well as jump. Charlie leapt some of the bushes as well and then disgraced himself by rolling in a muddy puddle.

'Yuk Charlie – another bath tonight for you, my friend,' Anna scolded him.

By the time they clattered back into the stable yard, Lolly thought her legs were going to fall off with tiredness.

'You did very well. Fudge is quite wide and her short stride is very bouncy. I hope you're not put off her for life,' Emma said as she lifted Lolly off the little pony's back.

'Oh no, she's gorgeous. I wish I could keep her,' Lolly gave the hairy pony a big hug around her neck and whispered into her ears. 'Thank you darling Fudge.'

'Bye Emma, bye Fudge, bye Smartie.' The girls waved as Emma trotted off down the drive.

Supper was lively with the children recounting their forest ride to Grandpa.

'Our friends think we're SO lucky to be able to spend our holidays here,' Beth sighed 'But it would be lovely to have ponies at home.

'Perhaps you'll be able to come for the whole school holiday again. Now, we have something else to look forward to as the day after tomorrow is SHOW DAY!' exclaimed Granny. 'Let's head upstairs now to sort out your best riding clothes so they're ready for Saturday. Oh, and Beth, I rang up the Pony Club District Commissioner today and she thinks her grandson's old jodhpur boots might fit you.'

13

'Oldest clothes today,' Anna said at breakfast. 'We have to shampoo the ponies and you and Charlie are bound to get wet too. Thank goodness it's sunny so they'll dry quickly. Then we'll clean all the bridles, saddles and boots until they gleam.'

Wearing old T-shirts, shorts and welly boots, carrying sponges, buckets, an old tin bath and old towels, the three sisters trooped across the garden behind Anna to the stables.

'Better bring Charlie's lead, we don't want him wandering off after his bath getting dirty again,' Beth said, turning to run and fetch it.

The horses had finished their buckets and were back

in the field dozing in the morning sun. Bracken and Summer were lying down with Magic standing guard over them, her hind leg resting and her head drooping sleepily.

'It almost seems a shame to wake them,' Anna said. 'Let's get everything ready first so they can be lazy for a little longer.'

She organised her work party.

'Niki, you fetch a couple of logs for you and Beth to stand on. Beth, please fill these buckets with water. Lolly, help me carry out the little table from the tack room, to put the equipment on.'

Lolly caught Charlie who was investigating something smelly in the field, and quickly clipped his lead onto his collar. Beth and Niki walked quietly into the field holding the headcollars behind their backs as before. Bracken scrambled to his feet as Niki approached but stayed still long enough to be caught.

'Good boy, thank you for not running away today,' she murmured in his ear.

Magic just opened one eye and yawned as Beth slipped the headcollar over her ears. Summer got up and followed as they led the ponies back to the stable yard.

'Not today Summer,' Anna said, closing the gate on her. 'You stay in the field out of our way.' She took some hay into the field to keep the big horse occupied.

'First thing to do is pick out their hooves as usual and give them a quick groom to remove any mud or sweat left from our forest ride yesterday.'

Niki turned on the hose and Anna instructed her to aim the water gently at Bracken's hooves, to give him time to get used to the feel of it.

'Get him wet all over,' she added as Bracken hunched his back against the cold water. 'Aim the water over his tail, starting near the bottom and working up to the top.'

Bracken squirmed again as the cold shower soaked through his tail hairs to his skin.

'Now Beth you do the same with Magic. Then rub in the shampoo, first with your hands then use the water brush on their manes and legs.'

The girls worked happily, flicking soapy water at each other and giggling as they worked up a lather on the ponies to wash away all the grease and dust from their coats.

'Magic's mane still looks grubby. Shall I do it again?' Beth asked.

'Yes, you'd better and her tail will need two or three washes before it's really clean. Don't forget to give her knees an extra rub too.'

Anna had brought a Thermos flask of hot water which she added to the cold in the tin bath, then, with Lolly holding his lead, she lifted Charlie up and plonked him in.

'Sit still, Charlie,' Lolly scolded, scooping up water in an old mug and pouring it over his long coat. 'We'll get just as wet as you if you don't stop wriggling.'

Charlie enjoyed the attention really and sat with a smile on his lovely face, letting Lolly soap and rinse his back and tail while Anna washed him gently, first his face, then she lifted each leg in turn, cleaning carefully between his toes and checking his long coat for burrs and ticks. They let Charlie get out of the bath before rinsing him off with the hose. He shook himself violently, spraying water everywhere and making the ponies – and the girls – jump and squeal.

'OK, Charlie, that was obviously pay-back time,' Anna laughed, skipping out of the way. 'Now Lolly will help you to dry.'

Anna gave Lolly a big towel with DOG written on it.

'Rub his face very gently, then work back the same way the coat grows. Carefully dry each leg and ask him to give you a paw, then dry between his toes so he doesn't get sore. Be gentle with his tail as well, he needs it still attached to his body.'

Anna had been keeping an eye on progress with the ponies.

'That's good, well done girls, now to sponge clean the ponies' eyes and wash out their noses.'

Once they all agreed the ponies were clean enough they were rinsed off with the hose. Niki and Beth towelled the manes before combing out the tangles, and windmilled the tails, gleefully spraying each other with flying drops of water, before de-knotting them with their fingers.

'Now we have three clean animals,' Niki stood with her hands on her hips and head to one side, 'but how are we going to keep them clean overnight?'

'Ah, good question. If you look in the black trunk in the tack room, you'll find lightweight rugs, bandages and old socks. There's even a dog coat for Charlie.'

Lolly had trouble deciding which way the coat went onto Charlie, who wasn't helping; he wanted to get dirty again. With Niki's help, at last she managed to strap it on round his chest and underneath his tummy.

Anna made fat plaits out of Bracken and Magic's tails, then folded them inside the cut off legs from old tights.

'When we undo their tails tomorrow they'll be lovely and wavy, just as if they'd been permed.'

Then she covered their legs using soft pads like cotton wool under the bandages.

'While they're still drying we'll plait their manes, before we put on their rugs. Use the white bands for Magic's mane and black ones for Bracken's. Put one round the bottom of each plait before folding it under to make a neat "bobble" effect.'

'We'll leave their forelocks until tomorrow so they don't rub them overnight, then French plait them. We'll probably have to redo some of the plaits in the morning but it'll be much quicker than starting from scratch.'

Beth and Niki worked hard trying to make the plaits even, but it was quite a time before everyone was happy with the results.

'Finished is better than perfect,' encouraged Anna when the girls became frustrated.

At last the ponies were dry enough to have their fly rugs on.

'Good thing these rugs cover their necks right up to their ears, and go under their tummies too,' Beth stood back to look at Magic. 'You can hardly see any of her white coat, she's all rug and bandages.'

'With luck they'll keep these on tonight so we won't have so much to do in the morning.'

'Shall we put them back into the field now, Anna?' Niki asked.

'Yes please, then we'll only have to check them this evening at feed time.'

Granny came to the stable yard to see how they were getting on.

'I need to take Beth to Mrs Dunlop's to try on johd

boots if you can spare her. If they don't fit we'll go to Morris's Saddlery to see what they have in their second hand department.'

Beth gave the washed, brushed and rugged Magic to Lolly to hold, and skipped off with Granny.

'Hmm, good thing I brought a clean pair of socks,' Granny said, surveying her dishevelled grand-daughter. 'Perhaps we should use a pony brush on your hair.' She laughed at Beth's horrified expression.

'Oh no, Granny, you can't,' Beth said earnestly, 'they're all wet.'

14

Niki thought the sun must know what an important day was dawning with yet another cloudless sky. She heard Anna get up and dashed downstairs, pulling her wellies on over her pyjama trousers to follow her aunt to the stables. For once, the ponies were not already waiting for breakfast but quickly trotted into the yard when they heard their buckets being prepared.

'I'll just take Summer across to Mervyn's yard for the day. You go and join the others for breakfast Niki. I won't be long,' Anna said leading Summer down the drive.

Niki was too excited to eat much, and Beth, white faced with nerves, also struggled to finish her cereal and was happy to let Minou lick the milky bowl. Lolly, who was always hungry, even had two slices of toast spread with Marmite.

'Poor Charlie has his rug on again. Never mind Charlie, it's not for long,' Lolly put her arms round his neck.

The girls rushed around getting in each other's way as they collected their grooming kits and tack to load into the Land Rover. Charlie was squashed into the boot along with the picnic, and the show jackets were carefully hung on coat hangers.

At last Granny asked, 'Got everything? Saddles, girths, bridles, hats, boots, Charlie's lead? Ponies loaded?' and to a chorus of 'yes, yes, everything,' they set off.

When they arrived at the show ground, Granny said, 'We'll park under this large tree. It'll give us some shade later.'

Charlie stayed in the car while they unloaded the ponies.

'Best Turned Out is always the first class so take off their rugs and bandages while I neaten a couple of plaits,' Anna said. 'Hold Bracken's head still while I plait his forelock. Now for Magic. Niki, brush a little oil on their hooves to make them shine.'

'Let me put the ribbons into your hair, girls. Straighten your ties and do up the jackets. I've put your gloves in your pockets. Do you need help with your boots, Lolly?'

Granny lined up the girls and checked them over from their hats to their toes.

'You all look fantastic. Those bows look a real treat, though I say it myself,' she said giving each child a careful hug.

Charlie wanted to investigate everything so Granny held his lead tightly as they walked with Anna and the ponies to the show ring.

Anna said, 'Niki, you go in first so Beth can follow with Lolly on Magic. You don't have to do much, just walk around the arena in single file with all the other riders until the judge – that's the lady standing in the centre – calls you in, so watch out for her to wave at you when she wants you to stand in line. This is all about cleanliness and looking smart, so chins up and smile. Judges always like to see happy riders.'

Anna gave them a last brush and they walked into the arena.

'Good luck; have fun.'

'Don't they look a picture? Those big bows in Lolly's hair are just so cute. Good thing she doesn't look like the mischief she is. And Niki's single long plait makes her seem so grown up. She's getting quite tall too,' Granny was having a seriously Proud Grandmother moment as she aimed the camera at the girls.

The judge didn't keep them walking round for long but quickly asked all the competitors to line up so she could make a detailed inspection. First she looked at each pony's head and checked inside their ears; then she ran her hand down their necks under the plaited manes to see how much grease and dust was hidden there.

She looked under their tails and even lifted hooves to make sure they had been picked out. She inspected the stitching on the bridles and underneath the flaps of the saddles to make sure the tack was clean and properly maintained. Then she stood back and took in the overall picture of pony and rider. Sometimes she asked a rider a question.

'Did you do the plaiting yourself?'

'How do you clean your tack?'

When she reached Magic with Lolly sitting erect but grinning from ear to ear, and Beth standing smartly by the pony's head, she smiled and asked who had managed to wash the pony so very white. Lolly spoke up before Beth could.

'My sister washed her with special shampoo which our aunt has for the white bits on her horse. Aunty Anna showed Beth how to plait and I scrubbed her legs and hooves. Then we wrapped her in cotton wool for the night. Our big sister did Bracken all on her own,' Lolly added, pointing towards Niki.

The judge's eyebrows rose and she smiled as Beth butted in. 'Not cotton wool, silly, gamgees under her bandages and her fly rug.'

The judge nodded, murmured her thanks and moved on down the line until she had looked carefully at all the ponies.

'Before I announce my decision,' she said loudly, 'I want to thank you for making such an effort this morning. Your ponies are a credit to you all and obviously a lot of hard work has gone into turning out both them and yourselves to such a high standard. You could teach the grown-ups a thing or two.'

'Now, because I know how hard it is to get a grey pony looking really clean and white, especially round the ears and hocks, I am going to ask Magic to stand forwards first.'

Lolly and Beth opened their eyes wide with excitement and even Niki grinned at them.

'Go on,' she whispered bossily. 'Walk forwards to the judge.'

The judge went on to place a skewbald second (his white bits were very clean too), then Bracken came third. Every rider was given a rosette and a quiet word of encouragement from the judge. Beth was asked to lead Magic round once with the others following before leaving the arena. Granny and Charlie were hopping up and down with excitement.

'Calm yourself Mother,' muttered Anna, embarrassed. The girls were beside themselves, laughing and talking at the same time.

'She asked how I cleaned the tack so...'

'She said we wrapped her in COTTON WOOL...'

'We've got a red rosette to match our ribbons...'

Beth hugged Anna. 'Thank you SO much for your help, thank you, thank you,' she said, hugging Granny and Charlie too. 'This is the best day of my whole life.'

'Hold on there, it's only the beginning of the day. We have lots more to do yet. Back to the trailer and let's see if we can find some bacon butties on the way.'

15

Breakfast had been hours ago and they'd been too excited to eat anyway, so the bacon butties were very welcome. On the way back to the trailer, they passed the dog arena where dogs of all shapes and sizes were waiting with their handlers.

'Is a class about to start?' Granny asked one of them.

'Quick, Lolly, finish your butty and hop off Magic. Dog With Waggiest Tail starts in five minutes. Just take off your riding hat and then you'll be ready.'

Anna took off Charlie's hated rug and quickly brushed his coat, paying special attention to his tail.

'There, all ready. Now, just walk around the ring with the others but don't get too close to them. Talk to

Charlie to make him wag his tail. Here's a dog biscuit to offer him if he needs encouragement. Keep one eye on the judge and listen to what he says.'

Lolly didn't have time to be nervous. She was still buoyed up by her previous success so she jumped off Magic, grabbed Charlie's lead and joined the other children in the ring with their dogs. She kept talking to Charlie who looked at her adoringly knowing what was in her pocket. He was so delighted to be out of his hated rug that he waved his tail all the time.

The judge took a long time choosing. Some of the dogs only had stumpy little tails and he thought Charlie had a slightly unfair advantage with his magnificent plumed tail, its white and black feathers swishing elegantly. Eventually he picked a little Dachshund with a long tail, then a Terrier with a short tail which never stopped twitching. Lolly's face was beginning to fall and she put her arm round Charlie's neck just as the judge called her into third place.

They dashed headlong out of the ring, Lolly being pulled by Charlie whose yellow rosette was tied to his collar. The family crowded around.

'Well done, Lolly. Good boy, Charlie.'

'Didn't he look handsome?'

'And he was so good.'

'I think he should have been first.'

'I really wanted Charlie to be first,' Lolly sniffed,

holding Granny's hand as they went back to the trailer. 'I still think he's the very best dog in the whole wide world, but third's good, isn't it Granny?'

'Of course it is, darling. After all, only two others were better than him out of a huge class.'

'Lead rein jumping next, so we'll leave Bracken with his haynet. You two girls had better come and watch so you know what to expect in your own classes,' Anna said, changing into trainers so she would be able to run with Magic. Granny tied Charlie to the car bumper to keep Bracken company, and once Lolly had put her hat back on and remounted, Anna led Magic to the jumping arena. There were about a dozen small children on ponies in the collecting ring, so Anna asked the ring steward to put Lolly's name on the waiting list and then they stood carefully watching the riders jumping their rounds until it was their turn.

Anna put her arm over Magic's neck, pointing out the course to Lolly.

'You've jumped much higher at home, both on and off the lead so there's nothing to worry about. Just make sure Magic doesn't overtake me. If I let go of her we'll be eliminated, and we don't want that to happen, do we!'

Granny found a straw bale to sit on and the sisters joined her, watching as each rider tackled the course. One little girl burst into tears half way round and was led out. Another was being led by her father who ran so fast the rider was bounced out of the saddle. One pony refused to have anything to do with the jumps and would not budge once he had entered the ring, so they had to give up too. Several riders completed the course, but some knocked down a jump or had a refusal.

'Why did that pony have a second go at that jump Anna?' Lolly asked.

'He wouldn't jump it first time so he is allowed a second try. But he's given 4 penalty points, the same as for a knock down,' Anna replied. 'Not many clear rounds yet,' she added quietly. 'If you're at all unhappy just yell STOP at me. But otherwise try not to shriek, laugh or shout.'

'No, not unless I'm falling off. Then I won't be able to help it!' Lolly answered seriously.

'Ready?'

'Yup. Ready,' Lolly answered as they walked into the ring.

'We have to wait for the bell to start. There it is...' Anna started to run, Lolly gave a kick and the pony trotted happily towards the jumps, her ears pricked. Magic jumped alongside Anna and then they were over the second almost before Lolly knew it.

'Steer left,' Anna puffed and Lolly pulled on the left rein, kicking with her legs so the pony would follow round the corner. They had practised so much that she knew what to do and just kept jumping level with Anna.

'Clear round,' Lolly shouted to Niki and Beth as she came out of the arena. 'Did we win?'

'Not yet,' Anna said, breathing hard. 'They'll raise the jumps a bit and all those with clears will go round again, against the clock. So I need to get my breath back.'

Only six riders were called into the collecting ring for the timed jump off, and this time Anna and Lolly were second to go. The first rider trotted fairly slowly and cleared all the jumps again.

'We'll have to go a lot faster than them. Hang on to the saddle with one hand and steer with the other if you can,' Anna instructed her niece.

The bell rang; Lolly gave Magic a kick and she cantered towards the first jump so close to Anna that the lead rein was slack. Over they went with Anna running as fast as she could to keep up. Magic seemed to remember the way and turned almost by herself, while Lolly held onto the saddle tightly with one hand, holding both reins in the other. Breathless and red faced, Anna collapsed giggling as they left the ring.

'And I thought I was fit,' she gasped. 'Fit for nothing after that. Well done Magic, you were a star. Lolly you were brilliant.'

'Sorry, Anna, I think I kicked you as well as Magic.'

'Easily done but not to worry, I'm used to bruises.'

They watched the other ponies but only one – led by a teenage boy – looked as if they were as fast. Sure enough, when the places were announced Lolly on Magic was second with the teenage boy's rider coming first. The winners lined up to collect their rosettes and smiled shyly admiring each others' ponies; the boy told Anna he had almost 'bust a gut' trying to beat her.

'A blue rosette this time. Now Magic has one red, one blue and Charlie has a yellow,' Lolly was thrilled as she hugged Magic's neck. 'And Bracken has a yellow too.'

'It's Beth's Minimus Jumping next, so someone hold Magic while I walk the course with her,' Anna said.

Beth was pale with nerves, watching carefully as she waited her turn.

'Wait to hear the bell before you start,' Anna reminded Beth as she entered the ring. 'Good luck. Keep thinking and enjoy yourself.'

Beth trotted round until she heard the bell and then she headed Magic for the first jump. The pony was quite keen and jumped it easily, breaking into canter as they headed for the second, where she turned sharply and Beth was nearly unseated.

'Oohh,' gasped Niki, watching.

Magic slowed down, waiting until Beth had regained

her balance and they finished the round without any more problems. They came out of the ring at a rather smart trot, with Beth happily smiling. Again, they watched the other riders who had mixed fortunes.

Several knocked a pole and one fell off. One pony dumped his rider and wriggled under the ropes before cantering towards his trailer with the red faced child chasing him. Several ponies refused a jump, because their riders held the reins too tight, jabbing them in the mouth. A few jumped round without mishap.

'There are about 6 clear rounds. The jumps will go up but no higher than you've done at home, Beth. This round is timed so cut corners rather than going faster. Magic will probably remember the course so you might have to steady her. Don't worry, she's a clever pony and will look after you!'

Beth trotted in with confidence and asked Magic to canter as soon as she heard the bell ring. She remembered to sit forward in a strong jumping position this time and the pair raced over the ground, cornering sharply between jumps. As they cantered across the finish, Beth was sitting up and trying to stop.

'Circle her away from the entrance,' Anna called. 'Don't leave the ring until she's come back to walk.'

'Gosh, what a good round,' Granny and Niki clapped as they finished, while Lolly jumped up and down, shouting 'Wow, she's won, she's won.'

'Not yet, Lolly, we won't know 'till everyone has gone.'

Beth waited on tenterhooks for the results, and was the only person who was surprised when she was announced as the winner; they had been flying!

'And of course,' said Beth, hugging Magic's neck, 'she already knew the course so it was much easier for me.' She proudly rode into the arena to collect her red rosette. To her amazement she was also presented with a small statue of a horse with '1st Minimus Jumping' engraved on it.

Niki and Lolly walked back to the trailer each side of the champions, with both the rosettes fluttering from Magic's bridle.

16

'There's just time to have a drink before Niki's jumping class. Magic can rest now until the gymkhana this
afternoon.' Granny spread the rug on the ground for
the girls to sit on while Anna took off Magic's saddle
and bridle and offered her water in a bucket then
tacked up Bracken.

Niki nervously rushed around looking for her jacket,
hat and gloves before mounting. She rode Bracken
quietly to loosen his muscles and then Beth held him
while she walked the course with Anna.

'These jumps are quite small and straight forward,
so just keep him moving with your legs. Are you nervous?' Anna asked.

'Yes, just a little bit,' Niki replied.

'That's normal, but you'll be fine. Watch the others before you go in.'

Anna gave Niki an encouraging pat when it was her turn.

Bracken knew his job and cantered steadily over the jumps, so that by the time they were half way round Niki's nerves had disappeared and she started enjoying herself. She had a sticky moment when he jumped the first of the double rather too long and had to put in a short stride before the second, nearly unseating her. After all their practising, however, it was not surprising they finished with a clear round, qualifying for the timed jump off. Beth and Lolly clutched each other tightly as they watched.

'A clear round. Well done. You were so calm. Bracken was magnificent.' The girls crowded round excitedly, patting Bracken as Niki came out of the arena.

As usual, there were a few falls and refusals, as well as jumps knocked down, but once again there were several clear rounds, some looked really fast.

'Only go fast if you feel safe. Cut the corners rather than galloping, but most importantly, enjoy yourself,' Anna told her niece.

Niki nodded and rode Bracken with determination into the arena for her timed round. She had watched the others carefully and decided to be cantering before the bell so she could save a second or two. Bracken happily picked up speed, cutting corners, with Niki leaning over his neck encouraging him.

'Come on, hup, left, go, go, hup, right, hup, go, go,' she urged as they went faster and faster.

'It's going to be close,' Anna said, as Niki crossed the finishing line. 'She was clear, and fast enough for a good placing but the class hasn't finished yet.'

Both Niki and Bracken were puffing hard so walked around to cool down away from the riders still milling around in the collecting ring. Beth called her back when the last round had been jumped.

'Two riders after you knocked down jumps, so you might be placed. Come on, they're about to announce the results.'

They waited anxiously, hardly daring to breathe, as the commentator started at 6th place, then 5th (still no Niki), 4th, 3rd (Niki's fists were clenched) 2nd - Niki on Bracken.

'You did it. Hurrah. Yippee!' Lolly and Beth danced, clapping and cheering as Anna encouraged Bracken with a stunned Niki back into the ring. She took her place next to the winner who turned to her, saying 'That's a good pony you've got there. I don't think I've seen you at any other shows, have I?'

'This is my first one. But of course Bracken has been

to lots with my aunt,' Niki replied, patting her pony's neck.

'Gosh, well done; we had to really motor to beat you,' the boy told her. 'Are you up for doing a lap of honour? I go first and you canter behind me then all the others follow us,' he explained. They set off with their rosettes fluttering between their teeth, Niki laughing as Bracken put in some happy little bucks.

It was a very over-excited group who returned to the trailer. Beth and Lolly were still dancing.

'How many rosettes is that now?' Lolly tried to count.

'A red for Magic and a yellow for Bracken. Then another yellow for Charlie. A blue for Magic in lead rein and a red for my jumping class,' Beth counted on her fingers.

'Don't forget your statue,' Lolly reminded her, 'and now a blue for Bracken again. That makes... oh, LOTS.' Lolly gave up.

'But best of all is you have a rosette from every class you've entered. And we still have the games this afternoon,' Anna reminded them.

'We'll have our picnic lunch after Charlie's Dog Agility class,' Granny decided. 'So we'd better head back to the dog arena now.'

17

Leaving Bracken and Magic relaxing with their haynets in the shade of the trailer, they all walked with Charlie and Beth to the dog agility arena. Sitting on straw bales they watched the first competitors tackle the course. Beth put her arm around Charlie's neck and whispered in his ear.

'We're going to do this together, Charlie, so watch and listen to me as you won't be on the lead.'

'Remember to wait for the bell to start and plenty of praise in a light voice but your commands loud and clear. OK, go for it ...' and with a gentle pat for both Beth and Charlie, Anna sent them into the ring.

Charlie looked up at Beth with his ears pricked and his tail swishing.

'Good luck Beth, good boy Charlie,' Niki and Lolly called as Beth led him into the arena.

Shaking with nerves, she rested her hand on Charlie's head as they walked towards the start. Her first 'sit' was too quiet and Charlie just stood looking around.

She took a deep breath and shouted 'SIT'. Charlie looked at her in surprise and sat.

'WAIT,' her voice was gaining confidence; Charlie watched her closely. The bell rang and Beth shouted 'FORWARDS', as she ran towards the first jump. Charlie pranced after her; 'OVER', and he flew over the jump.

'Good boy. Now, BEND.' He weaved through the poles as Beth waved her hand in and out keeping level with him.

'UP,' as they reached the see-saw, 'Steady, steady, WALK,' she told him as he carefully walked up the see-saw, and waited while it swung down before bounding off the other end. The next obstacle was the tunnel and Beth ran towards it shouting 'THROUGH, THROUGH,' as they had practised on the lawn at home. Charlie was quite big but he shot through and was quickly out again before Beth had caught up with him. He bounced around her asking where to go next and she pointed to the table.

'UP and STAY – LIE DOWN,' she commanded and he jumped up and lay, tongue lolling, wagging his tail madly, eyes firmly fixed on Beth. She held her hand out in the 'stay' position whilst she counted. 'One and two and three and four and five.'

Then she yelled 'UP'; Charlie bounded off the table and they raced towards the next jump, which he cleared before she had a chance to tell him what to do. He was going so fast he nearly overshot the final jump, but Beth called just in time so he skidded over it the correct way and they raced across the finish line with Charlie bouncing up at Beth, licking her face and tripping her over in his excitement.

'Oh, I couldn't keep up with him,' she wailed as she fell breathlessly into Anna's arms.

'He was so fast and so good,' Lolly and Niki had their arms around Charlie making a big fuss of him while he licked everyone and kept bouncing around.

'Quiet, Charlie, down,' said Granny as she tried to clip his lead back onto his collar.

'Some of the smaller dogs find the bending and tunnel easier so they may be faster overall,' Anna reassured Beth. 'You did a really good round, especially as this is Charlie's first time, and I think you're probably one of the youngest handlers even though it's a children's show.'

There were still quite a lot of dogs waiting to run, so

they returned to the car for lunch. Granny had made all their favourite sandwiches: egg, Marmite and lettuce, and coronation chicken. She buttered currant buns and laid out drinks and biscuits. They tucked in happily, chattering and recounting the morning's adventures. Lolly spread out their rosettes on the ground.

Bracken and Magic dozed in the shade and Charlie had a long drink from his water bowl before lying flat out, panting, under the car.

'Anna, please can I borrow your mobile phone to tell Mummy how we've done this morning? I promised I'd let her know when she rang last night to wish us luck,' Niki asked.

The loudspeaker system coughed into action;

'The dog agility class has now ended, so would all competitors please come to the arena to hear the results.'

Beth leapt to her feet, anxiously grabbing Charlie's lead.

'Quick, quick, I mustn't be late,' she said dashing off, leaving her bemused family staring after her.

'I'll go and wait with her,' Niki said.

Handlers and dogs milled around outside the arena, straining to hear the results. Beth's hands twisted in Charlie's thick coat as he leant against her legs. Niki waved at her, holding up both hands with her fingers crossed for luck.

'There were so many competitors we split the class into Large and Small dogs. In the small category, 6th place went to...'

Beth, in the middle of a crowd of barking dogs, couldn't hear the results but just watched as dogs and their handlers lined up in the arena. She was startled to find Niki pushing and shoving her;

'Go on, silly. Move. You've only come 4th in the large dog class. Go and collect your prize.'

Beth's grin was nearly as wide as Charlie's as they came back with a green rosette proudly tied onto Charlie's collar.

'Fourth? Oh well done, kiddo,' Anna exclaimed. 'You both deserve it after all those bumps and bruises. Now, no time for lollygagging; we need to get ready for the gymkhana.'

'Beth, you and Niki tack up Bracken; bring your hats too, there won't be time between the classes to come back to the trailer.'

Anna helped Lolly to saddle up.

'Time to ride like the wind, young 'un.'

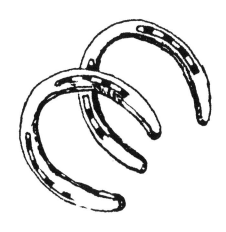

18

'Here we go Lolly. There'll be two heats then a final for each race. Everyone draws a numbered ball out of a hat which tells them if they're in the first or second heat. Then the first 3 from each heat go into the final.'

Lolly put her hand into the hat. 'It's a 2,' she said sadly.

'That's good. It means we can watch the first heat.'

The starter's flag came down and the ponies began the bending race. Some of the leaders ran very fast, bumping their small riders around in their saddles and one young child burst into tears. Then Anna led Lolly in for the second heat.

'Remember, only shout if you are falling off or want

to Lucy. 'Granny's here too. Your pony's lovely – what's she called?'

At last the judge came forward holding out the red rosette.

'Well done,' she said handing it to Lolly. 'You were very brave to go so fast.'

'The rest of the races will seem slow in comparison,' they agreed as they drew heats for the second game.

'Mug race now. If the mug falls off the pole shout NO to me. Don't shout if it stays on,' Anna coached Lolly while they waited for their heat to start.

Again the flag went down but this time Anna kept Magic to a trot so Lolly could pick up the mug from the first pole and then put it down on the fourth. Back up to the second post where Lolly grabbed the next mug then down again to leave it on the fifth pole. Round and back to pick up the final mug and then a careful trot to the end pole, accurately slamming the mug down.

'Hang on,' yelled Anna and again they raced back to the finish line, leaving all three mugs on their new posts.

Their main rivals, John and his sister Lucy, were also in the finals. Lolly fumbled her second mug and they had to stop to pick it up, letting Lucy get ahead. Again the final canter to the finish was fast but this time John and Lucy were able to stay in front.

Lolly was upset. 'I let you and Magic down,' she sobbed.

'Nonsense, of course you didn't. You still came second as others made mistakes too. Anyway, there are still two more races, so keep calm. We've practised loads so you know exactly what to do,' Anna comforted her.

The mugs were removed and replaced by cones with flags half way down the line of poles and an empty cone at the end.

'On your marks,' the starter called and lowered his flag.

Magic cantered forward with Anna running alongside; they slowed so Lolly could pick up a flag, then they dashed to the empty cone where Lolly had to lean over and put the flag into it. Back to collect the second flag and back to plant it. Then Anna grabbed Magic's mane and allowed herself to be galloped over the finish line.

Once more they were successfully through to the final; once more the arena was littered with exhausted runners, overexcited ponies and either jubilant or tearful small riders.

Again the final was a race between Lucy and Lolly and this time Lolly won. Anna was looking distinctly hot and breathless as they prepared for the last race.

She gave Lolly, who was speechless with excitement, a thumbs-up sign.

'Lucy's not in this heat,' she said, 'and we only need to be in the first three to qualify for the final so we'll keep an eye on the others but not race to win. Think of it as a practice.'

So, when the start was signalled they set off steadily. Lolly jumped off to grab the balled up sock. Anna helped her back into the saddle and they slowed to drop it into the bucket before picking up speed to cross the line.

'Phew. We did just enough and I saved some puff for the final,' Anna lent against a sweaty Magic as they waited for the next heat to be over. Sure enough, Lucy was through to the final too.

'Hang on tight to the sock once you have it, and I'll lift you into the saddle. Then lean as far over as you can to drop it into the bucket and watch to make sure it doesn't fly out again. Good luck, kiddo.' They both patted Magic as they waited for the flag to drop.

Off they went as fast as they could to the end of the row; Lolly threw herself off the pony as she slowed and grabbed the sock whilst still on her hands and knees. Anna bent and, holding the back of Lolly's johds, swung her up into the saddle.

They were off before Lolly had time to put her feet in the stirrups. She hung onto Magic's mane. Anna slowed as they approached the bucket and Lolly leant down, dropping the sock carefully while Magic stood still. Once she'd seen the sock stay safely in the bucket Lolly shrieked 'GO', grasping both the saddle and mane with both hands and still without her stirrups, managed to hang on until they were over the line when she finally slid right off the pony and sat on the ground, laughing delightedly.

Anna picked her up and hugged her.

'We won, we won, well done kiddo.' Magic hung her head, breathing heavily; Niki and Beth were laughing and crying and jumping up and down hugging each other at the edge of the arena; even Charlie was leaping around barking.

'The overall winner of the Lead Rein Gymkhana is Lolly Elliot on Magic,' the judge announced, handing Lolly a large red rosette and several smaller ones, and a small statue with 1st Lead Rein Gymkhana engraved on it.

'Who's up for a lap of honour?' Anna asked the other finalists.

'Fine.'

'OK.'

'Could we stick to trot please as we're exhausted!' several voices exclaimed.

A very proud Lolly completed the circuit in rising trot, rosettes fluttering from Magic's bridle.

Anna ran alongside, holding onto the pony's mane and letting herself be pulled along.

'Now Niki and Beth can do all the work while I have a rest,' Anna said, plonking herself down on the ground.

19

Anna gulped down some water and Lolly collapsed onto the ground counting her rosettes.

'One, two, three small red ones, one small blue one, one huge red one and a statue too,' she exclaimed in delight.

Anna helped Niki and Beth to ready themselves and mount.

'Go and enjoy yourselves. Remember the ponies know what to do so go out and have fun,' she said encouragingly.

The heats were drawn for the first race; Niki on Bracken was in the first with Beth and Magic in the second.

'That's good. It gives Magic another minute to rest,' Beth said, patting her pony's sweaty neck.

Niki urged Bracken forward to the start line and watched intently for the flag to be lowered. Leaning forward she yelled GO in Bracken's ear and he leapt into the air nearly unseating her. Fortunately he knew he had to bend and took the first few poles on his own. Niki soon regained her seat and control and remembered to swing him wide before the turn around the final pole so they were in the right direction for the return. She leant right forwards, pressing the reins against one side of his neck then the other to steer him, left then right, left again and they galloped over the finish line.

Beth was nervously hoping Magic would not leap forwards like Bracken as she took her place at the start. She heard Niki call to her to lean forward and then the flag was down and they were off. Beth started to enjoy weaving through the poles and kicked the pony into an even faster canter, crossing the line in second.

'Wowee. We're both in the final,' crowed Niki giving Beth a high five.

The six finalists lined up, with Bracken and Magic drawn next to each other.

'Good luck,' the girls whispered to each other as they watched the starter.

Niki didn't yell this time so Bracken didn't leap in the air at the start. He galloped down the line of poles, turned wide, then flew back without breaking stride once. Beth was determined not to be left behind and urged Magic on, following Bracken closely. She remembered this time to take the turn wide and Magic flew over the ground as they twisted back through the poles, trying to catch up to Niki who was the clear winner, with Beth a close second.

'Hmm,' the judge said as she handed out the rosettes. 'Don't I recognise that pony from the Lead Rein class?'

'Our little sister was riding her,' Niki answered. 'They have to share her.'

Beth and Niki were both in the first heat of the mug race. The poles were a bit taller than their practice ones at home, so Niki was able to pick up the mugs easily but Beth had to stretch out of the saddle from little Magic. Bracken trotted between the poles and was still quick, whereas Magic had to canter to keep up and they both finished in the first three so again were in the final together. Two of the riders in the second heat dropped mugs, and had to jump off to retrieve them and then remount before finishing.

'I do hope I don't drop a mug. Magic is far too excited to stand still,' Beth worried.

'Bracken is even worse. Just take it steadily, like I have to,' Niki replied.

This race needed accuracy rather than speed so the riders stayed in trot while they collected and deposited mugs onto poles. A couple of mugs fell off and the riders had to dismount to pick them up, but the others were all very close as the last mugs were placed onto the end poles and four ponies thundered to the finish line. Magic tried her best but Bracken and another larger pony were faster so Beth was third to Niki's first. Beth stood close to Anna at the edge of the arena while they waited for the next race.

'Magic tried so hard in the bending, now she feels tired,' she told Anna.

'Going slower will give you time to think. Sock race next – tell her to "stand" when you need to get back on, the way you did with Charlie. And Niki,' Anna turned to her oldest niece, 'Bracken is too excited to wait for you to mount, so hold the inside rein really short so he has to turn towards you rather than race off in a straight line.'

20

The girls rode to the start line repeating Anna's instructions under their breath. The sock race made Niki nervous as she knew from their practises that Bracken would only give her one chance to remount before he took off at speed.

Down went the starter's flag and they galloped full pelt to the end of their lines; several of the riders, including Niki and Beth, jumped off before their ponies had stopped. Anna had taught both girls to swing the ponies around at the same time as picking up the socks, so they were facing the right way when they remounted. Beth got her foot into the stirrup and hauled herself into the saddle quickly while Magic trotted quietly towards the bucket. She dropped the sock in without slowing, then kicked on over the finish line.

Niki was not quite so lucky as, with Bracken being taller, she had to make several bunny hop jumps before she could get back on. By the time she was properly in the saddle she hardly had time to sort out her reins before she reached the bucket and had to circle before aiming the sock into it. Fortunately Bracken's speed meant they still finished in time to be included in the final.

All the ponies were thoroughly wound up by this time and pranced around waiting for the start, backing up, bumping into each other and turning circles. Beth was grateful that Magic, being tired, stood quietly watching the starter's flag so she started straight. All six ponies were neck and neck as they raced to their cones, but Beth slipped as she jumped off which slowed her down collecting the sock. She yelled "STAND" to Magic who was jigging around. She managed to remount and they trotted to the bucket.

Niki was determined not to be left behind this time and also shouted "STAND". Bracken was so surprised he actually did stand still while she remounted. She caught up with Beth, and leaning down as far as she dared, dropped the sock into her bucket where it stayed. Bracken galloped for the finish, overtaking Magic.

One of the other riders had been ahead of Beth but had to turn back when his sock bounced out of the bucket.

The six finalists lined up for their rosettes, breathing heavily and rather red faced. This time Niki was second and Beth third again.

'Just the flag race to go,' Niki encouraged Beth, who was finding all the excitement a bit overwhelming. 'Bracken's getting really strong; I'm having a job holding him. Thank goodness we don't have to dismount again.'

This time Beth was in the first heat and Niki had to wait for the second. She walked Bracken around in circles to keep him calm as her sister went forward to the start. Beth urged Magic to canter to the flag which she picked up well, then they trotted to the far cone so she could put it in carefully. As soon as the pony felt Beth straighten in the saddle she cantered steadily back to the finish, well ahead of her rivals.

Niki's race also went smoothly although Bracken cantered between the cones rather than trotting and then galloped over the finishing line rather faster than Niki had intended. The finalists lined up on their heaving ponies; Beth was too tired to be nervous and was thankful Magic didn't have the energy to play up so they could trot through this race too. Bracken set off rapidly and Niki had to work hard to slow him down in time to collect her flag. One of the other riders was carted straight past her flag and had to come back from the other end of the arena. Another dropped her flag when she tried to put it in the cone and had to dismount to pick it up. Niki had Bracken on a really short rein by this time and firmly told him to "WAIT" and "STAND" while she pushed the flag into the cone.

Beth had trotted steadily to the far end with her flag, carefully ramming it into her cone. She had nearly caught up with her sister because Bracken was jiggling around, but when he saw Niki let go of the flag, he exploded into his fastest gallop yet, with his nose stretched out and his ears hard back. Niki didn't have time to check Beth was OK behind her, but just hung on grimly until they were over the line.

'I can't stop,' she yelled to Anna who was standing near the exit and managed to catch Bracken as he came charging towards her, completely out of control. Niki was clinging to his mane and nearly crying with fright. She was only too happy to let Anna lead her back to collect her rosettes.

Meanwhile Magic had managed to raise a final tired gallop and came in third with Beth grinning widely and patting her happily.

'Phew. I'm glad that's over. I'm nearly as tired as Magic,' she said collapsing forwards onto the pony's sweaty neck. 'Darling Magic. You're a star.'

All the riders hugged and patted their ponies, most of whom were far too excited to stand for the final presentation. Anna held onto Bracken who was looking forward to his lap of honour, but Magic's head drooped so Beth dismounted, putting her arm around the pony's neck.

The judge called Niki in as the overall winner.

'Congratulations. You've got a really fast, well trained pony there,' she said, presenting a large red rosette and a small cup suitably engraved.

Beth was third, which Anna told her was amazing against so many older children.

'It was all Magic, she looked after me so well,' Beth said as she burst into tears and hid her face in the mare's mane.

'Are you up for the lap of honour, Niki? I know Bracken will enjoy it but only if you want to,' Anna asked doubtfully.

'Oh I must – and I'm sure I can control Bracken because this time we'll be in front.' So Niki set off holding her large rosette in her teeth, letting Bracken enjoy his canter. He still put in a few bucks just to show he wasn't tired. Beth led Magic quietly out of the arena to be hugged hard by Granny and Lolly, who exclaimed over their haul of rosettes.

'It's a good thing we haven't entered anything else or we'd be accused of pot hunting,' Granny laughed. 'Well done, girls. I hope you've enjoyed your day.'

21

'If you'd like to stay and watch the senior games, Granny and I will take the ponies back to the trailer,' Anna said, knowing her nieces would enjoy watching the races now they knew how it felt to take part.

Niki tugged Granny's arm; 'Granny, we want to buy Anna a present to thank her for all her help this holiday. Shall we look at the mobile shops on our way back to the trailer or do it later?'

'Watch this class, and then we'll browse the stalls together before going home. We might even have time for an ice cream.'

Instead of leading Bracken quietly back to the

trailer, Anna shouted "gee up" and he burst into a canter, letting her vault onto him.

'Show off,' Granny called after her, laughing.

Beth was amazed as they watched the seniors gallop flat out. 'Gosh did we go as fast as that?'

'Bracken did and Magic was nearly as fast,' said Lolly firmly.

Niki realised how well they'd been taught, as they watched ponies racing back and forth with their teenage riders banging mugs onto posts, leaping off and running to the socks, vaulting on, sometimes dropping the equipment and having to turn their excited mounts.

'We're really lucky to have Aunty Anna to teach us and Bracken and Magic to ride,' she exclaimed.

'Ready to look at the trade stands before we go home?' Granny asked when they met up at the trailer.

Lolly held Granny's hand and skipped along, counting rosettes in her head, while Beth and Niki kept stopping to look at the horsey equipment for sale, making comments such as:

'Oh, look at that.'

'What is it?'

'Do you need one of those, Anna?'

At last Beth found a model of a china horse with a blaze just like Summer's which they decided to buy for Anna; a china mug with the head of a Border Collie for Granny and another one for Grandpa with a black and white cat just like Minou.

They were heading for the ice cream van when they were stopped by a lady dressed in tweed, who spoke in rather a loud voice.

'Hello there Mrs Elliot. I thought I recognised Bracken this morning but didn't have time to speak to you. Are these your girls? They did really well in the games this afternoon. I hope they're going to join Pony Club; we could do with them in our teams.'

'Girls, this is Mrs Dunlop, the District Commissioner for our local Pony Club branch,' Granny said. 'My granddaughters are only here for the holidays but perhaps they could join next year so they can attend Junior Camp.'

'What a good idea, and don't forget we have the indoor jumping show at Christmas which they could enter as temporary members. Get in touch when they next visit. Oh, and tell Anna we could do with her training our Prince Philip Team. She's obviously a brilliant teacher.' Mrs Dunlop walked away briskly, not waiting for an answer but calling "well done" to various children as she passed.

Beth and Niki helped to tidy away all the tack, water buckets and picnic while Lolly lay on the grass putting the rosettes into three piles.

'We'll write who won which and for what on the

backs this evening before we forget,' Granny said as, ice creams finished, they drove home.

Anna left the girls feeding the ponies while she went to fetch Summer from the blacksmith's forge.

'She was in the field with my old chap most of the day,' Mervyn said. 'I brought her in and gave her some tea so she's all ready for you. How did your young 'uns get on then?'

'Thanks so much for looking after her today, Mervyn. The girls did us proud; they were placed in all their classes and kept cheerful through a long day,' Anna replied.

'Can't ask for more,' he replied, giving her a leg up on to the impatient horse. 'I reckon they be chips off the old block, eh.'

Anna rode Summer bare-back to the stable. She whinnied loudly to her two friends, bouncing around so Anna had to grip hard with her knees to stay on.

'Whoa, steady there. Quick, open the gate so we can come in.'

'We've taken out their plaits and let them have a long drink. Bracken went out into the field and rolled over and over. I am glad I wasn't sitting on him when he shook himself afterwards,' Niki said.

'Magic's too tired to roll. But she still managed to eat her tea,' Beth said, gently stroking the little mare's neck.

The horses happily trotted into the field for a lively

canter, where they pranced, snorting through their noses, before settling down to graze.

'We've nearly finished; we just have to put away the traveling gear. Granny's already taken Lolly and Charlie back to the house to start supper,' Niki explained.

'That's great. So there's just the tack to clean before supper,' Anna said brightly.

'Oh no,' Niki groaned, rolling her eyes and making them laugh.

'Just kidding, it can wait until tomorrow.'

Later Anna put her mobile on loud speaker and the girls all talked at once telling their parents about their successful day. They were still chattering happily whilst having their baths and cleaning their teeth, recounting the thrills of the day even after they'd been tucked up in bed.

Gradually tiredness overcame them as first Lolly then Beth fell silent. Niki lay on her back with her arms under her head, and quietly murmured, 'What a fab summer with the ponies and everything. Tomorrow Mummy and Daddy will be here for their holiday. Then,' she sighed, 'it'll be time to go home and see our friends at school. And THEN it'll be Christmas and we'll be back to see the ponies and Charlie and everyone again. Can't wait.'

She yawned and her eyes closed.